Houses in the Fog

Saint John stories by Saint John authors

Houses In The Fog
First edition December 2019-11-09
Partridge Island Publishing Inc.
Saint John, NB, Canada

Cover Art and illustrations by Maryam Syed and Grayson O'Hearn
Editing by Sandra O'Driscoll and Megan Munn
Cover Font by Denise Bentulan
ISBN: 978-1-9990768-0-1

Foreword

"Houses in the Fog" began with the desire for some artistic souls to show their love of this wonderful gem of a city. The authors of these stories and the artists who created the artwork that accompanies each chapter are either Saint Johners by birth or by choice. How we ended up here doesn't matter. What matters is that we've found each other and now our words have found their way to you.

The artwork featured in the book were created by Maryam and Grayson. Every house is a stylized representation of the home upon which the story was based. We want to help our readers visualize the eclectic and wonderful architecture that can be found in the city while simultaneously protecting the anonymity of the homes. We love that Saint John has retained so much of its original character and hope to inspire the same sentiment in you.

We were tasked to create fictional stories surrounding the houses of our foggy city. As such, any names, characters, businesses, places, events, and incidents are either the products of the author's imagination, or are used in a purely fictitious manner. These houses are based on real houses, but the images have been rendered to protect the privacy of the homes' residents.

"Houses in the Fog" went from being an idea

around March 2019 to the final product you're holding in your hands at the end of November 2019. It was a labour of love for all involved. As if getting a writing group started and publishing a short story collection wasn't ambitious enough, in May 2019, we also established Partridge island Publishing, Inc.

This group, this company, and this book are all the results of countless hours given by everyone who could spare a moment. We have to give a huge thanks to our Editing Department: Sandra and Megan; the Art Department: Maryam and Grayson; our Advertising and Human Resources Department: Shannon & Amanda; and Greg, Head of Marketing and Social Media.

There have been superhuman efforts made by everyone that took part in creating compelling stories in weeks while at the same time, learning the ropes and doing jobs they have never done before. In just a few months we succeeded in turning all those ideas into edited stories with beautiful art.

These authors are part of Write Now Saint John, a writing group that was started in January 2019 by Chris, Shannon, and Amanda. Chris has moved onto other projects but his creative spirit and belief in the artistic community helped bring us together. Without him, it is doubtful this collaboration would ever exist. We thank him from the bottom of our hearts for being the catalyst for this, and future, projects. We would also like to thank John Gillis of Gilbert

Mcgloan Gills. Without his guidance, we would not have been able to take our idea for Partridge Island Publishing Inc. (affectionately known as PIP) from a dream into reality.

We hope you enjoy your literary wander through Port City by way of "Houses in the Fog."

Sandra O'Driscoll, Managing Editor

Megan Munn, Editor

Contents

Houses
in the Fog

Greg Sommerville

Greg A. Sommerville sounds like a pen name but he's a real person who is trucking through life as a full-time student and part-time working man. His goal is to get a job in the computer field and marry his super wonderful and total awesome fiancée, Amanda Evans, who is a co-author in this book and the helping hand to create his debut, the poem, "Houses in the Fog."

The city is old,

Cursed and Dying,

The youth, the lifeblood, leaving,

The houses, the ways, the money,

All of it, old -

Heritage, they call it -

Stagnant if you read between the lines.

The houses stand, mostly decrepit,

The heart has gone out of them.

Stone, wood, mortar, and forgotten memories,

The curtains, like eyelids,

Dark and heavily draped,

Unblinking eyes hiding their soullessness.

In a few decades how thin will the blood be?

How many will be from the city that holds them?

Who among them will cherish the lore?

Of The Three Sisters, Loyalist Burial Grounds, or Fort LaTour?

Will they know the warf-rats, Voc, or Harbour Station?

Times are changing -

It is as if the spirit of Saint John is lost in the mist,

Alone and adrift, like Houses in the Fog.

Sandra O’Driscoll

Just as Sandra, mom to Yesterday, the Italian Greyhound, knew she’d one day be a librarian, she also knew she was destined to write.

...And edit.

1908

The thump of the passenger ship jostled Fiona awake. After weeks at sea, the startling sensation of the sudden stop of forward momentum jarred her from her sleep. She peeked over the edge of her berth to where the young woman from County Limerick was nestled. After spending so many years in England, then France, she didn't realize how much she missed the sound of a pure Irish lilt until Siobhan said hello in her soft rural accent.

Fiona's County Dublin accent held overtones of a harsh East London cadence that was then softened with the rolling "r's" acquired during her years in Paris. The three blended together into a pattern of speech that was as bewitching and enigmatic as she was. "Siobhan, are you awake?"

Fiona's bunkmate rolled over and blinked. "Do you think we've arrived?" she asked, still sleepy.

"I would think so," Fiona replied and hurriedly got dressed. Siobhan did the same when Fiona went to the bathroom since their cabin was only big enough for one person to move around comfortably at a time.

Once they were both ready, they collected their luggage and made their way through the rabbit warren of hallways and stairwells. With each turn, they found themselves swept up into a larger swell of people, the mass of bodies and luggage getting more tangled at each corner. Heaving a huge sigh of relief, they made it out of the suffocating underbelly of the ship and onto the deck, joining the throng of passengers lined along the railing watching the sailors secure the ship to the pier.

A city shrouded in a thin veil of the ubiquitous fog that she heard tell of during the entire voyage. Having gathered everything before heading to the upper deck, they waited for their turn to disembark. From the deck, the city gave the impression they were on the stage of an amphitheatre. With the buildings and homes layered on the steep streets looking like the rows of seats, and the way the fog magnified every sound, Fiona felt as though she had stepped into a role without a script or direction.

Her fingers sought out the scrap of paper with the address of the boarding house where she was to stay and gently rubbed it between her thumb and forefinger like a talisman. After the first-class and second-class passengers disembarked, the two women walked past the pile of steamer trunks and crates being unloaded from the ship and joined the line. The process through immigration was slow, but Fiona was patient. Having already immigrated to two different countries, she was well versed in the process and coached Siobhan as to what she should and shouldn't say.

The process was arduous; no matter how often she'd gone through it or practiced her responses, it was nerve-wracking. Though she could anticipate what might be asked, she couldn't take an easy breath until her papers were stamped and she was waved past the immigration official. The experience never got easier but Fiona was hoping that this was where she would finally settle and build a life. After years of working toward her goal of becoming a fashion designer, she allowed herself the smallest spark of hope that she finally might turn her dream into a reality.

Fiona waited on the other side of the door and it wasn't long before Siobhan emerged. They made their way from the city's port of entry toward King Street, which seemed to be the main street of the bustling city. They stopped at the top, on the edge of King's Square to admire the buildings surrounding the beautiful green space with the two-storey bandstand. They turned around to take in the panoramic view of the city. With their suitcases set in the grass by their sides, the women hugged and promised to stay in touch. Having one familiar face in a strange place would be a great comfort to them both.

Fiona watched her new friend pick up her case and cross the square, heading toward the Loyalist Burial Grounds. When Siobhan dipped down the hill and out of sight, Fiona picked up her own carpet bag and hard-sided case and started off in the opposite direction.

Standing at the top-most corner of the square, she observed the old cemetery Siobhan had walked through. It was nestled in a hollow, the old stones looking like craggy teeth- tilted and splintered. Having just left Paris, a city built upon hundreds of year's worth of history, Fiona found herself quickly enamoured with the charm and unique pieces of the tangible past of Canada's oldest incorporated city

She continued on for a few more minutes before finding the boarding house on the corner. True to the directions, she couldn't miss the church across the street from it. Its stone edifice made for an imposing presence, which was a feat given the city was rife with places of worship, and steeples punctuated the skyline like candles on a cake. As she climbed the steps, she finally began to acknowledge the aches and tiredness of the trip.

Mrs. Monaghan opened the door. "You must be Fiona," she smiled. "Welcome, dear!" She stepped aside and ushered her newest boarder into the foyer.

"Thank you for taking me in, Mrs. Monaghan," Fiona said. "When I asked acquaintances in Paris, your name always came highly recommended." She set her luggage on the carpet by her feet and looked around. "I could hardly believe my luck that you had a room available."

Mrs. Monaghan smiled. "I treat all my boarders as

family. To think you're still struggling back home." She tsked sadly, looking at Fiona. "Is it truly as dire as it seems?"

Fiona nodded sadly. "I'm afraid so. We're all still struggling and there's not much for a girl, let alone one with 6 older siblings, so I left home when I was 16."

Mrs. Monaghan looked at the young woman standing in front of her. "My dear, you can't be more than 20. You will have to tell me more about yourself once we've gotten you settled." She gestured to the suitcase. "I've put you in the large bedroom at the back of the house, if that suits."

"That sounds lovely, Mrs. Monaghan. I'm sure I'll be quite comfortable," Fiona assured the proprietress.

She followed the older woman up the wide staircase. The dark mahogany railing complimented the forest green thick-pile carpet and burgundy wallpaper. Sepia photographs were sprinkled along the wall up to the second floor. Mrs. Monaghan showed Fiona the bathroom she would share with the other boarders, and then headed to the door at the end of the hallway.

The rear bedroom ran the width of the house and offered a tiny sitting area to the left. There was a comfortable wingback chair nestled in the corner to the right of a large window, which provided Fiona with a view of the Bay of Fundy. On the other side of the room, opposite the door, the window to the right of the single bed overlooked the city and out to the harbour. Having lived in landlocked places her whole life, Fiona was enchanted with the idea of being able to watch the ebb and flow of the tide as the ships come and go.

"I'll leave you to get settled then," Mrs. Monaghan said. "Tea is at half-six each night. There are 4 other young ladies currently in residence, so you will meet them this evening. Is there anything more you need?"

Fiona looked around and shook her head. "I think I will be fine now. Thank you, Mrs. Monaghan," Fiona smiled and placed her luggage on the bed. "Can I help with anything for supper?"

The older woman waved the question away. "Don't you worry about that." With that she closed the door with a soft click.

Fiona turned back to her bag and the case on the bed. She opened the valise and lightly ran her hand over the collection of ribbons, lace, silk, and other treasures she had gathered during her travels through the years. She pulled out the scraps to gaze at the spools of silk thread laid on their sides lining the bottom of her case and the jar of buttons in a wide variety of shapes, sizes, and colours. The sum total of her wealth lay spread out before her.

She carefully repacked the items into their carrier and set it into the wardrobe at the foot of the bed. Turning to the carpet bag, she quickly unpacked the few clothes she brought with her then stowed it alongside the case. She placed her small travel clock on the night table set under the window. The hands had stopped so she would have to remember to wind and set it before bed that night.

The rest of the evening was spent pleasantly. The other borders were lovely ladies; two were also from Ireland, one was from England, and the youngest had just arrived from Montreal. Fiona's stories of her life and adventures kept them enthralled throughout their meal.

For the next few months, Fiona had to rely on Mrs. Monaghan and the connections the older woman offered to help Fiona find some work. Being an immigrant, and Irish at that, Fiona struggled. The city was full of women willing and able to sew; even the most sought-after seamstresses struggled to make ends meet if they relied on their needles and thread alone.

Despite Mrs. Monaghan's support and glowing recommendations to her friends, and her fellow tenants' frequent requests, Fiona continued to flounder. While she managed to pay her rent, some weeks she had not a spare penny to her name. The patching and simple repairs she did paid close to nothing and the factory workers and other working-class people sent her way by her landlady weren't in a position to pay her more.

She began to doubt her decision to move to Canada but unlike in the past, this time she couldn't see a way out. Having lived in Saint John for close to half a year now and seeing no increase in demand for her services, she still had no savings.

She spent hours hand-stitching the patches onto pants and skillfully repairing tears. Her stitches were so fine and precise that unless one knew where to look, Fiona's work was close to invisible. She spent the wintry months in the boarding house, thankful that her customers came to her. She couldn't imagine having to walk up and down the steep hills of the city in the cold weather. Ireland and England were both cold and damp but it rarely snowed, and while there was snow in Paris it was easy to avoid the hilly parts of the city. She was finding such was not the case in Saint John.

It was while she was letting out the seams of a dress that Fiona realized that she had something no other seamstress had in Saint John- her collection of ribbons and fabric. She spoke with her fellow tenants about her idea of offering to add subtle details to dresses and they all clamoured to be the first for Fiona's alterations. Fiona modified a dress for each of them just as long as they promised to mention the little detail Fiona added to revitalize the garment.

After receiving nothing but positive feedback regarding the small changes made, Fiona waited for Julie Devereaux, a steady customer, to drop off another dress. As a young newly-married client who appreciated quality work, Fiona thought she would be most receptive to Fiona's new service. The next time Julie came to pick up her dress, Fiona made the tentative suggestion of adding a bit of lace to the cuffs or piping down the front to accentuate the brass buttons. She had laid both options on the table and while her customer was wearing the dress for a final fitting, Fiona held the samples up to illustrate her ideas. Julie was thrilled. With the simple addition of some piping, her old dress that was on the cusp of falling out of style had been refreshed and given a new lease on life.

Fiona made the alterations and in a few days had the dress finished. Within the week of Julie picking up the garment, Fiona had a small surge in requests by ladies who could afford to spruce up a dress or two. By the end of the month, she felt like her luck had finally turned the corner and was heading in the right direction.

Fiona's business continued to steadily grow but she was ambitious. She knew she had so much more to offer the women of Saint John, and that the alterations, repairs, and embellishments that she was becoming known for didn't even begin to put her skills to the test. Each night she fell asleep creating a new bespoke gown for one of her customers or picking a component of haute couture and reworking it in a way that would be irresistible for a Canadian woman.

When she wasn't busy with commissions, she would draft her ideas, tweaking each creation until her vision was perfected. Each little model Fiona sketched was effervescent with optimism, exuding the confidence her creator was still struggling to find within herself. In Fiona's sketchbook, classic designs rubbed shoulders with avantgarde creations and fashions that had not yet jumped the pond from the Paris salons to Canada. Still struggling to find her place, sketching was her outlet and the one moment in her life where she was free to be her unapologetic self.

Fiona usually kept the book at home; the sketches too private to share with anyone and her ideas too precious to risk losing or falling into the wrong hands but that was exactly what happened. The last-minute commission for a new client took half the night to complete so when Fiona finally finished the alterations, she carefully folded the dress and packed it in her bag for delivery that morning. Unbeknownst to her, the book was nestled in the folds of the skirt.

Since the request was just for a simple embellishment, Mrs. Henley didn't need to try it on. When Fiona dropped it off the next morning, she was thrilled to see the maid who answered the door was Siobhan. The two women spent far more time than they should have catching up and when another maid came looking for the young Irishwoman, Siobhan took the folded bundle Fiona passed over and paid her friend. Exhausted, but thrilled to have reconnected with the young woman, Fiona barely made it back to her home before collapsing for a well-earned rest.

Having slept into the early afternoon, Fiona found it impossible to fall asleep that night so she reached for the notebook. Panicking when she couldn't find it, she tore her room apart. Stacks of loose sketches and pages ripped from catalogues wafted through the air as she ransacked her room. Clothes lay in haphazard heaps, her garments in one pile and the commissions left by clients in another. She sat on the edge of her narrow bed, waves of nausea rolling through her as she attempted to quell her panic. It never left her room so where could it have gone?

Overcome by the magnitude of her loss, she succumbed to the tears that she had fought back since her first few weeks in Saint John. She felt naked and exposed- those illustrations were never meant for anyone's eyes but her own and now they were lost in the ether- little orphans absorbed into the fog.

Fiona's spirit had rebounded from countless tragedies, some small and negligible, others life-changing, but none as catastrophic as this. She barely managed to get through her tasks; in fact, the only solace she had was when she had a needle or fabric in her hand. She worked to forget, and for a while that was enough.

The pain of her loss lessened over the course of days and weeks but never to the point that she felt inspired to pick up her pencil and resume sketching. Her little models stopped appearing in gorgeous new creations, and the details that once made Parisian fashion so enchanting lost its allure. Even her flare for picking the right embellishment was beginning to fade. She was no longer a creator.

Fiona had resigned herself to a mediocre and lacklustre life when she received another commission from Mrs. Henley. Fiona made her way over to the stately home on Germain Street to discuss Mrs. Henley's latest request.

Fiona had little hope for this appointment. What was once a successful business had steadily dwindled as she struggled to meet her clients' expectations. Known for her unique style and visionary approach to fashion, how could Fiona continue creating when it felt like her tiny muses she captured on paper were at the mercy of the person who had found them?

She walked into the morning room where Mrs. Henley was seated, a book was tucked by her elbow. A yellow strip of paper jutted out at a jaunty angle. Fiona gasped when she saw her sketchbook.

"My book!" she cried, her knees wobbling dangerously.

Mrs. Henley smiled and stroked the cover. "I thought it might be yours," she said. "My maid found it and gave it to me." She opened the cover and gazed at a beautiful sketch of a sleek gown.

Fiona closed her eyes, picturing that little figure. Etched in pencil, her mind could see every accent adorning the bodice and each tuck and dart of the peacock blue silk. She surreptitiously wiped tears that leaked from under her eyelids before opening her eyes.

Mrs. Henley closed the book and held it out. "My dear, I am so sorry to have kept it for so long but your creations are breathtaking. It was only this morning that I was able to decide which one I want you to make for me." She gestured to the makeshift bookmark.

Fiona held the book between both palms, needing to steady her hands for a moment before opening to the page indicated.

"I'd like the dress on the left side," the older woman said. She gestured for Fiona to sit in the chair beside the desk. "I need a new gown for the annual gala at the Royal Kennebecasis Yacht Club and I want something that will stand out." They looked down at the rendering of a layered creation with a hint of a train and a daring amount of exposed skin. With her figure and flawless complexion, Fiona couldn't imagine a more ideal woman to wear such a bold design.

"I would be honoured to make your dress for you," Fiona replied, already busy planning the pattern and picking out the perfect fabrics and details. Fiona spent every waking minute she could spare on the dress. At each fitting, Mrs. Henley grew more excited as she saw the dress take shape. When it was time for the final fitting, it was difficult to say who was more excited. For Mrs. Henley, it was the chance to be noticed and admired but for Fiona, it was the opportunity to finally make her dreams a reality.

It was fortuitous that Mrs. Henley ordered her gown for the festivities at the yacht club in 1909. After the overwhelming success of Mrs. Henley's haute couture, every woman wanted to be dressed by Fiona. By that Christmas, Fiona was sure she had single-handedly been responsible for every dress on display at the Union Club's holiday gala. Her treasured collection of fabrics and accents had long ago run out, save for a few pieces that she was keeping for herself. Luckily though, by this point her reputation was established in town.

After 2 years of designing and creating dresses and customized styles for the upper crust of the city, Fiona was ready to open up her own boutique. She wanted her own space to create and sell her designs. She began looking for a shop but met with resistance when it became known that she was a single woman looking to start a business on her own. Bankers didn't know what to do with such an intrepid woman and no one wanted to lease their property to her.

Fiona refused to give up. She continued to work out of Mrs. Monaghan's boarding house when doing simple repairs, but those were far and few between now that she was spending the majority of her time making house calls and designing bespoke creations. It was at one such appointment that Mrs. Brousseau asked about Fiona's plans. Fiona shared her struggle to find a suitable place to rent. Her client met Fiona's gaze in the mirror and promised she'd speak with her husband that night. It just so happened that he owned property close to the waterfront and was looking to rent one of the ground floor spaces. "It would be simply perfect for you," Fiona's client assured her.

And it was.

It wasn't long after that conversation that the rest of the pieces fell into place. Fiona looked around the empty storefront on Prince William St., one of the brick- and masonry-fronted shops, and sighed with happiness. With the ink still drying on the lease she signed, she looked at the narrow but deep store and started imagining how she would design the space.

She imagined bringing the haute couture and salons from Paris to Canadian women. She missed the beauty and art and culture of Paris at its peak of the Belle Epoque and it was time to put what she learned from the great Parisian designers to good use. Standing in the empty shop, Fiona thought about how far she'd come in the scant few years in a new country. Her friend Coco Chanel had just started making a name for herself in Paris; it had only been a few years since she had opened her store. Now it was Fiona's turn.

Amanda Evans

Amanda has spent most of her life in fantasy worlds, either reading them or writing them. In 2019, she has turned a dream into a reality. She is a founding member of both
Write Now Saint John and Partridge Island Publishing, Inc. and is a debut author in "Houses in the Fog." As every reader knows, all good stories are a series. Along with planning a wedding to her Prince Charming and biggest fan, Greg Sommerville, she is also looking forward to taking part in the second volume of the 'in the fog' collection and setting out on independent quests to publish a novel or two.

The Girl in the Summer Dress

She was shivering; the girl in the flowing summer dress standing in the wet, heavy snow of early spring. The night she was defying, in her light dress, was newly born and a few dark streaks of navy blended into the heavy black velvet.

Maryanne saw her from half a block down the street and her heart ached for the young girl. She couldn't see the child's feet but she felt certain that they were dressed in delicate shoes to match the knee-length light-pink dress, patterned with red roses, white daises and yellow daffodils. This was not the first night the wisp of a girl with long blonde braids had stood outdoors. This was the third night, at least, that she had been forced out into the cold. Tears clawed their way out of the corners of the older woman's eyes. "Child," she called. There was an accent in her words, more noticeable now that she was speaking louder, trying to catch the girl's attention as she walked towards her. Her heavy black boots made loud squishing sounds in the slush.

As child turned and faced Maryanne, her eyes grew wide with panic. Her twin braids flashed side to side as the girl looked about trying to decide which way to run. Maryanne picked up her pace, trying not to run where there was a chance of ice hidden below the opaque covering. The girl held no such reservations, and before her would-be helper could get any closer than three houses away the girl darted sure-footed and swift across the treacherous grounds. She disappeared into the dark yard and was out of sight by the time Maryanne had reached the spot where she'd been. Frustration knotted her stomach and she cursed in a language unknown to these streets.

Maryanne turned slowly, the night now dark enough that the street lights were coming to life. Her eyes lit upon the old church with its open field and traveled upwards to the cross that topped it. She said a word to the God that should be watching out for those so close to His home. Then in bitter defeat she headed homewards. It was her home now, but only through marriage. Her husband was the latest in a long family line to own the only brick building on the street other than the church itself. It was a sign of the family's close ties to the church that those that built it generations ago were allowed to use the stones. Everything else was wood and nothing else was quite as nice. That was the first thought that she'd had when she'd come here a scant few months ago, a year maybe; her bitterness was too overwhelming to let her think of anything else.

"David," She called softly, her accent made the name sound more like 'Day-fed'. There was no laughter now. Her husband was either not home or still not talking to her. He'd been mad at her the night before when she'd come home, her face masked in tears as she told him about the child that she'd seen. After she had seen the girl a second time, she had told him she was going to call child services on the people that lived there. He had been livid at her declaration, his voice raised to lift the rafters as he forbade her from doing any such thing. Her outrage and fear had filled her face with another wash of tears, but rather than comfort her he had grabbed his newspaper, the one that he'd let fall when she'd come in, and he left the room without a word.

"Are you home?" she asked, but the house remained silent.

She tugged off her heavy boots and quietly hung up her jacket on the peg as she listened for sounds of someone else around. Slowly she went through the rooms on the main floor, through the hall then the living room. She went to the dining room, and being empty she stole quietly into the kitchen. Her plate was in the sink waiting to be washed, but his was still covered with aluminum foil and trying to hold some heat in the cooled oven. The jumble of emotions that flooded through her were wild and ever-changing - before she could even try to grasp at one it was gone, replaced with something else: anger, indignation, humiliation, shock, sadness, guilt, anxiety, disappointment. The emotions burned hot, staining her cheeks and her forehead, the angry blush burning away the pretty daintiness of her pale complexion. It worked its way down her neck and spread like eagle’s wings across her chest.

"I will not be treated like this." She spat the words out, filling the wonderfully scented room with venom. Her limbs trembled and she lifted her chin, and fought down the urge to throw things before stomping out of the kitchen. Up the flight of stairs that brought her to the second floor of the beautiful house, she strode to her room, flinging the door open and letting it crash into the wall. It made a lot of noise but did nothing to cool her anger.

It didn't take long for her to grab the small travel bag and start filling it with the things she would need for her sojourn to a hotel. She knew there was one by Fort Howe, she couldn't remember the name, Keddy's tickled her mind. It didn't matter, she needed to get out of this house, away from her husband, at least long enough to decide what she was going to do next. She filled the bag with enough supplies for a couple of days then fought to zip it closed. The house was still empty as she stomped down the stairs. She stopped in the foyer to put on her boots. They still held some of the chill from her earlier travels, but she ignored it and grabbed her coat, buttoning the big coin-like buttons and muttering to herself as she did so.

The sky was dark as pitch except for the bright puddles of street light that illuminated her way. She was at the end of Douglas Avenue before she even thought of calling a cab, and now it was too late. The hotel was only a few blocks away so she kept walking, the cool air beating back the heat in her skin and the exertion helping to vent her anger.

The hotel doors opened as she walked up to them. The light greeted her, as did the clean, glossy floors, the thick area rugs and the gentleman that was standing behind the counter. His face wreathed in a smile as he looked up from the thick ledger he'd been working in.

"Good evening ma'am," he greeted and moved the book under the lip of the counter. She gave him a shy smile, making her face look younger than her almost 30 years and free from the cares she carried.

"Good evening yourself," she replied, striding over to the counter and putting her bag on the glossy floor. "I'd like a room."

The wide veranda was as welcoming as open arms. The door was brightly coloured and cheerful. Maryanne faltered. This house did not look as sinister as it did at night. It no longer seemed the kind of place that would turn a child out to freeze to death. Maryanne hurried across the porch and rapped heavily before she lost her courage.

The noise was loud and intrusive in her ears - demanding and rude. Her hand fell and twisted with the other one awkwardly in front of her belly, and a part of her hoped no one was home so she could come back and start this over again later.

"Coming," the voice was soft through the door.

When the door opened, it framed an older lady. Pin-straight gray hair fell shoulder length making her look gaunt, her lips were thin but showed no lines of either smiling or frowning. She was an uninspired woman, probably nearing 70. Thin stick-like fingers and a sensible, drab brown wool dress didn't help her look any less forgettable. The only interesting thing about her were her eyes, a softer blue than any Maryanne had ever seen in a person, a colour painters called arctic.

"Yes?"

Maryanne pulled herself from her observations. "I'm sorry to disturb you ma'am," she started, her words tumbled out thick with her accent making her cheeks pink in embarrassment.

The woman's face changed ever so slightly, bemused by the bumbling woman. "How can I help you?" she asked after a moment of watching her visitor shuffle.

"I'm Maryanne Fraylan," she introduced herself, and to her surprise the womans' face became colder at the sound of her married name. The Fraylans had been members of the church - diocesan bishops, bishops, priests, even down to alterboys for as long as the church had been standing. “I'm the wife of the dea-” She stopped and corrected herself, “the new minister,” she added remembering that he'd been promoted in the last two months.

“I am aware of the family you married into,” she said with a tone icier than the chilly air.

“I'm trying to get some information about a child,” Maryanne blurted quickly, trying to appeal to the woman though she didn't give the impression of being motherly. The hatred was palpable and venomous, and Maryanne could see in the woman before her a harpy that would throw a child to the cold.

“A child?” the lady repeated. “I don't know anything about any children.”

“I've seen a little girl hanging around this area for the last few nights and I'm trying to help her.” The older lady showed little interest in what she was saying. “She's wearing a summer dress, a knee-length-”

The older woman's skin faded until it was the same shade as milk and her hand tightened into a fist. “A summer dress...” the woman repeated, cutting Maryanne off. “Please leave,” she said angrily, backing into the house. Maryanne moved with her, in step as if performing a choreographed dance.

"Please, I want to help her!" Maryanne begged.

"Help? How dare you!" Like a light switch had been thrown the woman changed. Gone was the bitterness of a moment ago. The hatred was gossamer thin compared to the wrath of the older woman standing before her now. Gone was any frailty of age.

"Who do you think you are?" she hissed. "Coming around here and getting into things that you know nothing about! That 'child' you saw," the woman advanced, her steps echoing despite her small size," was my twin. You're seeing a ghost, and before you go around harassing victims, why don't you look into your own family and see how you can 'help'!"

Hours later, alone in her hotel room, Maryanne couldn't say for sure which stung more: the seething hatred and accusations flung at her or the slap that had landed on her cheek before the raging woman left her abandoned on the porch. Wracking sobs came loud and clear through the closed door.

Maryanne had stumbled, shocked, along the street she'd called home. The red handprint on her cheek had refused to be cooled by the damp March breeze. She wandered the street, looking at the houses that lined it. She looked at her own home - the one that had adopted her and had taken her in because of her husband. The stone walls were formidable, strong and ever-lasting, like the God of the men that had sired David. It stood solid, aloof, and uninterested in those around it, like it was better than all the others. That begged the question that tickled her mind, *if a house could believe itself to be above everyone else, then how could the people that live inside it feel any different?* Following that line of thought, she mused,*what dark secrets hide behind the wall of stone? More importantly, what secrets hid inside the walls of flesh inside that house?*

The cold chased her from the street and her feet took her through the part of town her husband had derisively called 'Indian town'. He had told her that this area had once been booming and beautiful, but all she saw as she walked were the homes that were so close to a church, but the poorest of the poor that she'd seen in Saint John. Some were barely better than shacks. It looked as though they were huddled together for warmth and security. There were more boards for windows than glass.

She wandered for a while longer, stopping at the department store in Lansdowne Plaza to buy some supplies she'd forgotten in yesterday's dash. Dusk was heavy in the sky when she returned to the hotel and made the arrangements for a few extra nights. She missed David terribly. Since they'd met they had barely been apart for more than a day or two and never when they were angry at each other, but she wasn't yet ready to face him.

It wasn't early, but neither was it late when Maryanne walked through the doors of the Saint John Public Library. The smells from the food court mixed with the sounds of the splashing fountain and the screams of the children playing in the little playground below. Not for the first time she had to wonder where her future was going to go from here. She touched her stomach, still slender for all that they had tried to build a family.

She pushed past the thought, shoving open the doors and found peace. No matter where in the world one goes, a library is a library:the sound of a lot of people trying not to make a lot of noise, the soft lights, and the smell of books. It's a piece of home anywhere you travel and no one, no bad day, and no revelations can take that away. She walked over to the gently curving front desk.

"Can I help you?" the librarian asked, her face helpful but not entirely interested.

"I'm trying to get some information on Saint Peter's Church," Maryanne stated.

"I know that place, my parents used to go there." The librarian's face lit up a little and Maryanne could tell she wasn't as old as the dress and vocation made her seem: late twenties, early thirties at most, likely close to Maryanne. "I'm not a churchgoer though. What are you looking for?"

“The woman on the street told me that there were some ghost stories originating around the Church. My husband is part of the ministry. I thought it would be an interesting topic for one of his sermons.” She lied with an ease that would have shocked David, or the David she thought she knew.

“There are quite a few news articles about the churches around here. The people of Saint John seem to love their God almost as much as they love their coffee,” the librarian said with a sardonic look.

Maryanne grinned back, having seen the number of churches and coffee shops around the city when she'd had her first tour with David's family a few days after moving here. “Where should I go to find the papers?” Her eyes roamed up the stairs and around the side of the counter. She didn't look behind her; she'd seen the colorful pictures on the walls and knew that that alcove was the children’s wing.

“Are you comfortable using the microfilms or do you prefer paper?”

“I prefer paper, but it would probably be easier using the microfilms,” Maryanne replied after a few moments.

“A woman after my own heart,” the librarian replied with a smile. “I'm Bethany, but you can call me Beth,” she said leading the way towards the opening at the end of the counter.

“Maryanne,” she introduced, pacing along on her own side of the counter.

“The microfilms are stored upstairs,” Beth said, leading the way. The stairs were wonderful to look at - the banister was glowing wood and glass and the steps had a heavy rubber tread. The view from the top was even more beautiful looking down. It felt like this was a mansion, not a home for books. She couldn't stop the smile. “I know. This place takes my breath away every day,” Beth said noticing her pause. “I'll go get the canisters. How far back are you looking?”

“How far back do the records go?”

“It gets spotty at times, but we have some papers from shortly after the city was incorporated.” She didn't even try to hide the pride in her tone.

“Let’s go back to about 1890,” Maryanne suggested, quite unsure what she was looking for, but a century back seemed like a good starting point.

“This is going to be quite the project,” Beth said with surprise.

“I have a few days and little else to do while he's working.” She shrugged but even she could hear the ring of truth and bitterness in her words. She smiled to hide it but Beth's eyes were a little wider than they had been a few moments ago.

“Grab a seat, I'll be back soon.” Maryanne moved to the rail and looked down on the people below her, letting the scene dull the aching that was starting in her chest. It didn't take long before Beth returned with a large case of tubes. Carefully, she walked Maryanne through how to use the equipment, then brought her a pen and paper and left her to her own devices.

Hours poured away like water from a faucet as Maryanne worked, stopping for half an hour to grab something to eat before getting right back to it. “Finding what you're looking for?” A voice asked over her shoulder. Maryanne ignored it, her hand moving quickly to scrawl out the information from the newest article she'd found. The voice came again, this time with a tap on her shoulder. "Finding what you’re looking for?" Beth asked when Maryanne finally turned from the light of the screens.

"Yes, actually, much more than I thought I would." Maryanne's voice held excitement. "I just have another decade or so to go."

"Then I'll look forward to seeing you tomorrow," Beth countered smoothly before Maryanne could try to get back to her work.

Maryanne looked at her watch, her eyes widening in surprise, "Heavens, that late already?"

Beth smiled. She knew that feeling of getting lost

in research because the hunt was paying off. "I'll shut down the machine. Have a good night, Maryanne." Maryanne smiled and gathered up her puddle of papers that had taken over her desk and had spilled onto the empty one beside her. The two women worked in quick silence as the minutes ticked until the library closed for the night.

The tea she was drinking was awful by the standards of what she grew up with, and bad by the standards of what she was used to at her husband's home. To make it even worse, it had grown cold while she worked at the small desk in her hotel room. She reached out and sipped the brew without thought, a habit of a lifetime. The pages that she had written while at the library were neatly piled in front of her and they were tragic and telling. There was an alarmingly large amount of people that had gone missing or died in close proximity to that church - men, women, and children. It seems that someone was 'missing' or 'passed away through unusual circumstances' every eight years or so.

She had even found the article about the old woman from yesterday. After the day she had, she was shocked to realize that the visit to the old woman had been only yesterday. The article spoke of twin girls, aged 10, that lived on Harvey street. They had been playing hide and seek around the church. Annabell was hiding and Laurie was trying to find her. After an hour, Laurie had gone home thinking her sister had given up the game but Annabell wasn't at home either. That night, the search party found the little girl at the bottom of a set of steps that led to the church's basement. It was believed that she slipped, but Laurie had insisted that she had checked that area earlier. Since there was no sign of foul play, the death was written off as a tragic accident. From Laurie's reaction, Maryanne was positive that she still believed it was something more sinister.

These stories, in the context of the city's history, were easy to dismiss, but when they were compiled together, they painted a dark and sinister picture. Maryanne pushed herself out of the hard wooden seat, her rump numb .She needed to move. She chewed her lip as she paced the room, trying to work out what her next step would be. She wanted to go back to the library and finish her research. She was worried; the next roll of film would include the information from the time her husband had come of age and started working in the church: *what if the stories continued?* she thought. She wanted to call him, to tell him she missed him, and to ask him for his side of the story, but she wanted the facts more.

The night wore itself into its darkest hours by the time she climbed into her cold bed, physically ready for sleep even though her mind was still flopping around like a fish out of water. Her plan was simple:

tomorrow she would go to the library again and she would finish the last decade. Once she had her notes in proper order she would call him and make arrangements to meet him for supper, somewhere public, to talk to him.

The library was noisier today than it had been yesterday, and Maryanne could hear the sound of over active children as soon as she walked in. The security guard at the desk by the doors smiled in greeting and rolled his eyes at the children, giving a small shrug. She smiled back and pressed on to the counter. Beth wasn't in sight, and a slight frown tugged at her lips.

"May I help you?" The librarian called to her. She was older than Beth by a decade or two but she looked slighter and more the typical librarian with a tight bun, glasses, and lips that could purse and give a stern lecture easier than they could smile.

"Is Beth here?" Maryanne asked. "She was helping me yesterday."

"Bethany does not work on Wednesdays, but I assure you that I can be just as helpful." The librarian's words were curt and clipped. Maryanne missed Beth's smile.

"I was working on the microfilm machine. I'm looking for local newspapers for the past 10 years." Maryanne told her quickly when the edges of her eyes started to tighten.

"I understand." She grabbed a small pad of paper and a pen. She wrote something with quick, hard motions and then ripped the page to give it to Maryanne. "Take this to the desk on the second floor and Mr. Romanive will be able to assist you."

Maryanne took the paper and nodded that she understood, and before she could even gather the saliva to say thank you the woman was well on her way along the desk away from her. A little shaky, Maryanne started up the stairs feeling as if she'd just taken an exam and was found wanting. "Mr. Romanive?" she asked softly when she was at the desk.

"Gregore," the small man with a big smile returned, looking up from the book he was reading with a sheepish look. "How can I help you?"

Maryanne's shoulders relaxed and she gave a small grin back at the man, passing him the sheet that she'd been given. "I need help getting some microfilms."

Gregore Romanive read the words on the paper. "I see. Do you know how to use the machines?"

"I think I do. Beth-" she caught herself with a tiny cough. "Bethany showed me yesterday."

"I thought you looked familiar." His grin widened

and he stood. He wasn't tall; they were the same height although he looked big, strong and bulky. He waddled a little when he walked, not like a fat man would, more like someone that rode horses. Maryanne's own uncle Frederick had walked like that; he'd raised and trained horses for as long as she could remember. "I'll meet you at the machine. Are these all you need?"

"Yes, I believe so," she agreed, then realized she didn't know what was on the paper, just some codes. "I'm looking for the last 10 years of local newspapers." He nodded and then whisked himself away and left her to find herself a work station.

He held up two rolls in one large hand. "Here you go," he said a moment later, having made much better speed than Beth.

"Thank you."

"Not a problem, do you need anything else?" The words were sincere.

She patted the cheap portfolio she was carrying today, a purchase made yesterday from Pascal Emerson. "I should be fine, but if I do need help I'll call."

"Not too loudly I hope, this is a library." He countered with a little chuckle as if he used that line a lot and never got tired of it. She graced him with a grin, only half-forced, and he took his leave.

Maryanne busied herself setting up the machine and got back to the task at hand. Two and a half hours later she came back up. The scratches on the legal pad were much fewer than they had been yesterday. Almost overnight it seemed things had changed. The church, and the area itself, were no longer in the news, at least not negatively. There were no strange disappearances, no mysterious deaths, no church organized search parties. Nothing.

Quiet as she could be she packed the films into their tubes and gathered her papers. The only sound was the loud grumbling in her stomach which called the attention of an old man at the table close by. She gave him a shy look and her face reddened. "Here," she said softly to Gregore, passing the tubes over. "I'm finished."

"Already?" he asked, looking at the time.

She nodded, "Thank you."

"You are certainly more than welcome. If you need anything else, let me know." His words and face showed pleasure that she'd completed her work.

"I will," she promised and then turned and headed down the stairs. The entry way was quieter, the kids from earlier had gone while she was working and the library was again at the noise level it was meant to be. Outside of the library was a bedlam in comparison. She took the shallow steps a few at a time and looked across the open space, letting herself get lost in thought. Food. Then she'd call her husband.

She dithered, hummed, and hawed as she tried to choose her food. The food court was small but she made the decision drag. Try as she might she couldn't make it take forever, and 45 minutes later she was back up on the main stretch leading to the library standing in an old-fashioned red phone booth, quarter in hand, ready to make the call. Her fingers shook, but she deposited the coin and dialed the number.

"Hello, Dorothy, can I speak with David, please?" she said into the mouthpiece when a prim sounding secretary answered. "Sure, I can hold."

She placed her forehead against the cool glass pane and worked on breathing in and out slowly to keep the anxiety down. It had only been four days, but it felt like years since she'd last spoken to her husband and a world of information had come to light since then. "David speaking." David's voice filled her ear, rich and warm, thick with charisma and able to captivate an audience. She loved it. It melted her heart to hear it again.

"Hi, sweetheart," she said softly, the thin words having to wend their way around the thick emotion blocking her throat.

"Maryanne?" he asked, his voice hitched, but still lovely. "Where are you? Why did you leave? I've been going crazy with worry!" She could hear the genuine worry in his tone.

Anger flooded her. He hadn't cared so much when he'd just up and left during their fight. "That doesn't matter," she told him, breathing deeply to strengthen herself and let the anger melt. "We need to talk."

"We can talk at home, over supper," he told her, taking it for granted that she would do as he bid.

"No. We can talk during supper, but I don't want to go back there yet," she told him, finishing with *if ever* in her mind.

"Whatever you want, dear." She could hear him shuffling things around. "I'm sure we can work things out. But whatever you want, we'll do," he muttered. He was trying to placate her; she'd seen him do it often enough with parishioners. "Where do you want to go for supper?"

Maryanne shot a look around, trying to find some inspiration. She hadn't thought that far ahead. "Keystone Kelly's" she blurted. It was the closest restaurant she could see.

"Keystone Kelly's?" he asked, she could hear the cocked eyebrow. "To sit and talk?"

"It was highly recommended," she lied.

"Uh huh." He didn't believe her, but she'd shown him a side he didn't know existed when she up and left and he seemed more than willing to do what it took to get her back. "So Keystone Kelly's at 5?" he added.

"That sounds good," she agreed. "I'll see you then."

"Yes, you will. I love you, Maryanne," he said in that rich chocolate voice.

"I love you too," she agreed and hung up the receiver. Three deep breaths, then four, then another half dozen before she had herself back under control. She swung the door open and walked calmly back to the library. She had her information, her questions, her determination, and now she had to put it together in a way that would get her point across.

She skipped the stairs this time, going across the wood floor and onto the carpet. Finding a window spot overlooking the harbor, she dove into her work. The weak light from the window was filtered through the glass, after fighting hard to be useful. It was quarter to five by the time she was ready to wrap up for the night. She stopped in the bathroom for a few minutes to freshen up and made her way to the restaurant.

The interior of the restaurant was dim, but it didn't take Maryanne long to find David. He was sitting at a table in one of the secluded corners, his storm gray suit was only a few hues darker than the clouds out the window. She loved that suit on him. He saw her as she walked towards his table and his smile was like the sun. He rose to meet her, a quick kiss on the cheek the only sign of his affection. He took her elbow and led her to the table, holding the seat for her.

"I missed you," he said, the longing in his words mirroring the longing in her heart.

The food was neither good nor bad, but it was quick and the price wasn't exorbitant. They chatted and laughed like newly wed lovers until the waitress gave them their teas. Then the air of the date died.

Maryanne pulled the sheaf of papers out of the bag and passed them to him. She remained silent for a few moments and watched his eyes dance across her pages and the genial smile faded the farther he went. On page three of her neat handwriting the color started to drain and his hand shook as he picked up the cup to take a drink.

"David, what is this?" her words were not harsh or demanding.

"I.. it's ... coincidence?" He stumbled, putting the pages down as he proposed the words they both knew were wrong.

"David, don't lie to me. I know you better than

that," she insisted with a sigh.

"Can we go somewhere more private to talk?" His words were soft and there was a catch as he fought the tears that were wavering in brown eyes. She nodded somewhat reluctantly. "Thank you," he said with earnestness, and then pushed himself out of his chair to settle the bill with the server. She gathered her papers, trying to decide on the best place to go that would be 'private'. Home was not an option.

By the time he returned, it was obvious to her that their options were non-existent. "Let’s go back to the hotel," she offered with a sigh that he didn't miss.

The walk back was short and quiet, or as quiet as it could be when walking along the overpass as cars zoomed by. The hotel loomed before them long before they crossed the brief patch of grass to get into the parking lot proper.

"This is where you've been staying?" he asked her as they walk quickly under the stone portico.

"It is," she agreed, but didn't elaborate. Their feet slapped the glowing floor and Maryanne returned the smile of the man at the desk, but didn’t stop to talk. Leading her husband towards the pair of elevators across from the indoor pool’s doors, the ride up was short and strained. David's hand twitched to catch hers. His eyes caught hers in the mirror.

Her room was a corner one and rather small. She let him precede her, turning on the light in his wake. He took in everything; it had a bed, a desk, a chair and a mini fridge. The dresser-cum-tv stand took up most of the main wall. The window gave a view but no light now that the night had fully fallen.

"Are you ready to talk?" she asked as he turned to look at her.

David's chest heaved as he took a deep breath before wilting. He sunk down into the chair. Maryanne tossed the bag with the incriminating documents onto the end of the bed, close to where he sat.

"My Grandfather called it the Story of the Stones," he told her slowly after a few more heartbeats of quiet. The words were soft, he spoke like he was telling her a story he'd read in his youth. "The people of the church are people first, no matter how much they pretend that they are not." He looked at her.

“Over the years, my ancestors started to believe that they were superior to those in the flock. It wasn't unusual for them to 'test the sheep'." She could hear his disgust at the words. "They would create opportunities to allow the parishioners to prove that they love God above material possessions, money, or desires. Humanity often fails and those people, those stories, are the results of those that failed."

"How?" she asked, moving to sit on the bed, needing to sit. It was worse than what she had thought.

"Poison, adultery, torture," he stated with a shrug and the tears started. "It was immoral," he told her. "I refused to do it, but no one else did. I didn't know how to stop it, to stop them and I wasn't good enough, pure enough, to always rise above the bait." The tears were coming in earnest now.

"The scar on your back?" she asked, remembering the puckered blemish that he'd blamed on a fall on the rocks when he was young. She wanted to ask him if it was a lie, but she didn't. The soft-hearted man she knew was breaking down in front of her eyes and that was answer enough.

The night passed in a long, grueling vigil of tears and a baring of the soul that seemed as if it should never have had to come from a man of God. By the time they had fallen asleep, curled up and clothed in each others arms, the decision had been made. He would be the end of his line that worked at that church. Today he would go, put in his resignation and they would sell the house, move away from the legacy of men who held themselves in stone castles and played God with those in wooden homes.

34 Years Later

Maryanne looked around the old library. She breathed in the scent of books, and the lack of scent from all the technology that now graced the library, hidden like thorns in a rosebush. She saw some changes, but she was hazy on how much had actually changed and how much was just forgetting what things looked like after more than 30 years.

This year her husband had retired from his job in a factory in Alberta and they had finally returned to the city of his birth so that he could face the ghosts that had haunted him since he left. He finally felt it was time.

He had been torn when a friend that had still lived in the city called him and told him that the church was closing its doors after 133 years. He wanted to come back then, to stand in the church and prove that it had not broken him, but after talking it over they had decided that it wasn't worth the emotional trauma. She'd blamed it on the expense of traveling and the inconvenience of having to fit it around work, but they both knew the real reason. He'd let the doors close without his presence.

When he was finally ready, they flew back to the city of sin and coffee. Today, their second day here, he told her he was going back to see it. She had offered to go with him to stare at the stone house and the old church and face his demons, but he declined. He felt he needed to do this alone, so he dropped her off at the market on his way to the North End.

She wandered out of the library, shaking away the cobweb of memories, old and new, and looked over the rail at the atrium. Here the changes were glaring. Gone was the food court and the shops that stretched way back like a labyrinth towards the back door and the stone garden. It was replaced by a museum. The fountain still spewed jets of water up into the air but the decorations were different. New stores stood where once the little playground stood. Keystone Kelly's was gone now. There was another steak house that could have been the same restaurant where they had had their life-altering supper, highlighting how somethings simultaneously change and stay the same. They had driven past Keddy's on their way in on the first night and found that even that had changed. It was Howard Johnson's Fort Howe Plaza now. They had opted to stay somewhere else on this trip.

Her purse vibrated. A hand, still pale and slender but showing veins below the skin and a looseness they hadn't the last time she was here, reached in it. She looked at the message on the face of the phone.

"I'm done. I have made peace. I am hungry." She smiled at the words with true affection and started towards the parking lot under the mall. She was ready to go to lunch, then they would head home. She was ready to be home; he was her home, no matter where he was.

Amanda Evans and Shani Dykens

...what would happen if two stories overlapped...

The Story Between

"Hey, lady, this is the square by the City Market," the bus driver called as he rolled to a stop beside the bank at the top of the hill.

The words pulled her away from her people-watching. It wasn't working as well as she'd hoped it would to chase away the tears that threatened to fall. The sight of a young couple walking along the street towards them was more than she could ignore; the full roundness under her dress showed she was pregnant. She watched them as they stopped walking so that the young man could put his hands on the woman's stomach. His face lit up. Maryanne could only assume he was feeling the baby move under his hands. She fought back a sob and started to rise. "Where's the library?"

"In Market Square," the driver replied, "Oh. I understand, not the square by the market. Market Square is the building down by the wharf, at the bottom of King Street."

"Uh, okay," Maryanne agreed, not really knowing what he meant but feeling silly. She pushed her way off the bus as the tears started to flow. The ground was jarring, and she stumbled, crashing solidly into a masculine form that was almost as hard as the ground she stepped on.

Ian was quick to put out a steadying hand. "Hey, are you okay?" he asked.

"Yeah..." she started, but the tears cut everything else from her speech.

"I don't think you are. Can we help?" He offered gently.

“Ian, lobster tails.” Essie reminded him, not so patiently, rubbing her pregnant belly. “Simmer, babe, they’re not going anywhere.”

Maryanne took a deep breath and let a tiny, watery smile grace her face. "I need to find the library." She looked from one pair of eyes to another. "I was told to go through the market and it’s at the bottom of King Street. Where is that?”

"We're going to the market anyway, Es wants a little something sweet from the bakery. I'm sure we can do a little detour before we go home."

"Are you sure?" Maryanne asked, her eyes again travelling between the two lovers.

"Of course," Essie added, joining the conversation. "So long as I get my lobster tail first. I've been craving one for days." She had called Ian first thing in the morning to ask him to bring her up here, forgetting that he had worked all night. He was grumpy, but he got over it quickly enough. They’d nap this afternoon to make up for it.

"A lobster tail at the bakery? Saint John is a very strange place," Maryanne stated, blushing a deep red when she realized how her comment might seem insulting. She'd been here long enough to know that this place had its charm, but it was confusing.

The young couple laughed. "Come on, my treat," Ian offered, starting off and pulling the two women behind him.

"A lobster tail is made from the flakiest pastry and filled with custard and it's wonderful. I might have to get two!" Essie said to Maryanne in a stage whisper, “Ian likes them too, but he’ll never admit it.”

"I heard that," he laughed.

"You were meant to." Essie laughed and continued talking with her companion. “Although he’ll probably stick to his Beaver Tails, they’re his favourite.”

Maryanne shook her head at the way the two younger people teased each other. Ian’s attentiveness to Essie reminded Maryanne of her own husband's caring ways when they were first married.

Despite herself Maryanne felt some of the gloom ease away. The three chatted amiably while they waited for the light to change, Essie leaning into Ian’s side. Ian was attentive, his hand always at her back or kissing the top of her head. He kept the lead once they started again.

Maryanne had seen the market before but she thought she could live here another 10 years or more before the newness of it wore off. The great inverted hull ceiling, the dozens of stalls carrying every type of thing she could imagine: meat, fish, veggies, dried seaweed treats.

She'd tried dulse but couldn't imagine it ever growing on her.

Essie rushed forward once they were inside the loud building, pulling them to the left where the bakery was. The bright glass cases showed sugary confections that looked all at once delicate. "Three please," Ian ordered, pointing to the baked goods so that Maryanne could see what she was getting before she got it. Essie tugged at his arm. He smiled indulgently at her before telling the server to add a cinnamon roll to his order. It only took a moment to ring up. He moved out to the little patio where customers ordered so the next customer could buy their bread. "Here you go, babe," he handed one to Essie. "And you..." he paused."I didn't get your name. I'm Ian and this is Essie."

"Maryanne," the quiet woman offered, taking the pastry. "Thank you." The first bite was buttery and flaky, and she felt like she was wearing as much sugar as she was eating. The second was sweet with great gobs of cream trying to make a break for it.

Essie and Ian were making just as much of a mess as they went down the aisle, moving around shoppers.

"What are you looking for in the library?" Ian asked, being the first to finish the treat.

"Ghost stories," Maryanne said behind a hand to keep her from being rude as she finished her pastry.

"Ghost stories?" Ian and Essie said together- one with a fearful expression, one eager. "For the past couple of nights, I've seen a young girl standing outside in the cold wearing a summer-dress," she started, tossing her used napkin in the trash bin when she passed one. "When I went to confront the parents but the woman who answered the door was in her seventies and said the girl was her twin, who died 60 years ago. She told me it was a ghost." Maryanne left out the accusations and the slap, they weren't important.

"For real?" Essie perked up, her voice raised in excitement. She almost dropped the rest of the treat she was picking delicately at.

"Yeah, and I've heard there are other stories like it in the area, so I thought it would be interesting to look up," she told the young mother-to-be. Her enthusiasm rising to match Essie's, she almost forgot why she wanted to know.

"Did you need help?" Essie offered and Ian paled a bit beside her. Essie loved ghost stories: the more ghoulish, the better. Ian hated this stuff, it seriously creeped him out.

"Uh Es, you know we have an appointment today, right?" Ian asked looking at her pointedly.

"Wuss," Essie laughed. "But he is right. Sorry, I really would love to help you research," she said truly apologetic.

"It's okay." Maryanne acknowledged. They had finished their lobster tails and made their way back outside where they followed King Street down to the lights at the bottom of the hill.

"What are you going to do with the stories?" Ian asked while they waited for the light to change.

A frown curled on Maryanne's pretty face, making it seem much more plain that it usually did. She hadn't really thought of a good answer for this. "I don't know, a book maybe, or some campfire tales," she offered,but the ideas were vague and her accent tinted the words. "I'll figure it out. I just knew that I wanted to get more information about the stories."

"That's cool." Essie said. She nudged Maryanne when the light changed and the trio made their way to the front door of Market Square.

“It would be nice to share them with others. It would be a shame to let all this knowledge go to waste,” Maryanne added as Ian held the door open for the ladies to enter.

They followed the hallway past some offices and a row of restaurants on their left then made their way up the stairs. When they reached the top, Essie turned to Maryanne and proudly said, "and there, boys and girls, is the library."

Maryanne's eyes traveled in the direction Essie was pointing, and sure enough the storey-tall books and the large word 'Library' confirmed her statement.

"Thank you so much for helping me find it," she said with sincerity, "and for the company, and the treat."

"It was our pleasure," Ian replied. "Good luck."

"Yeah, good luck with your ghost stories," Essie agreed, rubbing in Ian's obvious dislike of the topic.

"Thank you," Maryanne said again. "Have a good day." And with those words, she pushed away from the happy couple towards her goal, heard them in the background teasing and being teased, happy and in love.

Shani Dykens

Shani has been writing poems and love stories since she was a teenager, preferring to live in her made-up world where everything is always happily ever after. She didn't seriously devote herself to it until she was in her 40s though- she's a lazy romantic. After 15 years as a cake decorator, she hung up her oven mitts for the last time and published her first novel, *Kiss Me* in the spring of 2019. Shani is a founding member of Write Now Saint John, a local writers group and Partridge Island Publishing Inc.

45.3074° N 66.0163° W

(Co-Ordinates)

Present Day

Ian Bennett pulled up in front of the building that housed the modern condos and shut the engine off. He took a moment to study the glass and concrete structure before he got out of his truck, his eye immediately drawn to the top corner apartment where he had spent so many years with the woman he loved. The fog was thick today, so thick that he could barely see the windows, but he knew exactly where it was. Essie loved the fog and the rain. He hated it, too many years working outside in it, but she would always drag him out onto the balcony during the summer storms and ask him to kiss her. She always said it was perfect snuggle weather. She liked how the rain made her feel calm and peaceful. He didn't get it, but that was her. She was weird. She owned it and he loved her for it. With her, he never knew what to expect. She pushed his boundaries and made him try new things. She made him better.

He remembered the night they met, 52 years ago. It was between Christmas and New Years, and he had a couple of days off so he and some friends went to the mall and there she was, working at one of the clothing stores in McAllister Place. He spotted her from the back first. Oh man, her ass in those jeans, he'll never forget it. She had long blond hair- bangs spiked, as the fashion at the time dictated. She was like every other girl their age until she turned to look at him and her eyes locked with his. They sucked him in right away. Gorgeous deep blue eyes. He fell in love with her right then and there. She looked like an angel dressed in white and she took his breath away. He couldn't leave the mall that night without finding some reason to talk to her. He got her to take his phone number, scared to death that she wouldn't call. She did, and it was the best thing that ever happened to him.

They fell in love. Not just a regular, everyday, I-want-to-spend-my-life-with-you love. It was the all-consuming kind that felt like they had known each other before. Two halves of the same whole. She had their entire life planned out within the first month. She scared the shit out of him most of the time; he needed her to slow down, but she couldn't do it. She was all in from the moment they met, and she never wavered. Their life together was not conventional. They did some things that perhaps they shouldn't have, but they did them anyway.

They were so young when they got together. It was hot and fast and they couldn't keep their hands off each other. It was no surprise when Essie soon got pregnant. Their little girl was premature and spent months in the hospital. It was a stressful time, and they were too young to deal with it so they split up before their daughter turned a year old. They eventually moved on with other people, but they kept coming back together. By the time they decided that they should just be together, Ian's girlfriend was pregnant. Essie wouldn't let him leave. She made him promise to work it out with this other woman. He reluctantly agreed to find a way to spilt himself between his two families. It was wrong. They both knew it, but they did it, anyway.

Essie was unapologetic about the way she loved him, convinced that they were soul mates. He always missed her, but today it was harder. Today was the anniversary of the day she turned his life upside down and it happened right up there in that condo. It was painful to think about, but he couldn't help it. He had been without her for 20 years now, and it still seemed like yesterday.

20 Years Ago

Ian buckled his belt, glancing over at Essie as he pushed it through the last loop. God, he loved her. He knew he didn't tell her enough, but he knew she knew. He so looked forward to these stolen moments with her. She was the bright spot of sunshine in his life: always positive, always smiling. She sparkled like the sun on the water, and she made him happy.

It had been an incredible 48 hours. They hadn't spent this much time together since they were kids.

He would never have attempted it, but she didn't ask for anything, so when she asked for this, he couldn't deny her. He had a hard time saying no to her; he'd do anything he could just to see her smile.

He watched her as she nibbled on her lip and he had a feeling something was bothering her. He wanted her to tell him what it was, but after 32 years together, if he knew one thing about Essie, it was that she would talk about it when she was ready. It drove him crazy sometimes, but he had learned not to push. Essie looked up at him and smiled, but it didn't reach her eyes. She stood up from the chair and padded to the kitchen to get a bottle of water from the fridge. She leaned against the counter, struggling to get the cap off, and finally gave up, holding it out for Ian to open it for her. She did this often lately, saying that her hands were sore. They were just weak, a symptom of her disease. Ian had no idea about this, but he was about to find out.

He took the bottle from her, noticing that her hands were trembling ever so slightly. He wanted to ask her about it, but something in her eyes made him stop. She smiled her thanks, reaching into the cupboard for the bottle of painkillers. She shook a couple of tablets from the bottle and swallowed them with the water.

"Headache?" Ian frowned. She had a lot of headaches lately. Alice, their daughter, had mentioned her mother's frequent headaches to him.

She was worried and asked her father about it. Essie had always been prone to migraines, he'd just assumed that's what it was. He stood behind her, running his hands up her arms. He rubbed her shoulders, feeling the tension.

"Hmm," she screwed the cap back on the bottle and placed it on the counter. He turned her around to face him, wrapping his strong arms around her. Essie loved Ian's hugs, she always said he gave the best ones. His arms felt like steel bands and this is where she felt safe, loved. Of all the things she loved about Ian- his beautiful bottle green eyes, his dark hair that was always perfect, the way he was just tall enough for her to fit right under his chin- it was the way he hugged her that she loved best. He radiated warmth, this soft-hearted man. Ever kind, unconventionally romantic, unrelentingly fair.

"You need to get some sleep, babe. Or maybe I should send you to the spa for a day of pampering. You love the spa; how about it? You can take Alice with you. She could use a break from running after Jack all day." Their grandson was a busy child, running his mother ragged most days.

She smiled absently, shaking her head. "Have you got a few minutes before you have to go home?" Ian was supposed to have been at a union meeting out of town. He was due back today, just about an hour ago, actually. His wife would be waiting.

"Not really, I'm running late as it is. Why?" He

eased her out of his arms and stood away from her, feeling the loss of her soft body immediately.

Essie nibbled on her lip, something she only did when she was nervous. Her eyes were wary as she struggled to choose her words carefully.

"Es, if you wanted to talk, you should have said something sooner." A hint of annoyance crept into his voice.

"Yeah, I know." She needed this time with him, though, once more before she had to tell him goodbye.

"Can we talk about this tomorrow?" Ian asked as he looked around for his keys and wallet. He could feel the tension building in the room and he didn't like it.

"Ahh, not really. Ian...please." Something in her voice cut into him. It was raw, as if her words cut her throat as she spoke them.

"Essie, don't. If you're going to say what I think you're going to say, just don't." He wasn't up for this argument again. It was the only thing they ever fought about, the amount of time they spent together.

Essie shook her head, she made her way over to where he was standing. She stood close to him, close enough that he could smell her shampoo.

"Call her and make an excuse. I'll go into the other room to give you some privacy. I need to tell you something and it needs to be today, so please. I don't ask you for much, so can you please just do this one thing for me?” She tilted her head back, her hand on his forearm, her bright blue eyes pleading with him. He sighed heavily, he couldn’t say no. Those eyes of hers sucked him in every time. He nodded. She was right, she didn’t ask for much. He picked his phone up off the table, telling her he would go into the bedroom to make his call.

A few minutes later, Essie heard Ian’s footsteps come up behind her. She was standing at the balcony, looking out at the harbour. The building had been designed to look like the cruise ships that visited Saint John. As soon as Ian saw it, he had wanted to move here. They had chosen this corner apartment specifically for the view. Ian loved to watch the ships from their bedroom. They had spent hours laying in bed dreaming of someday going on one of the massive boats. Ian put his arms around her, pulling her back against his chest. He felt her cool fingers glide over his arms, her gentleness soothed him. He saw her cheek lift as she smiled at the solid feel of him behind her.

“Tell me what’s going on.”

“Let’s sit down.” Essie slipped her palm into his hand, leading him over to the buttery soft leather couch and sat down beside him. She studied the way their hands looked together, running her fingertips over his knuckles. Working man's hands. She remembered the nights she spent digging metal splinters out of them when he was too exhausted to do it himself. Ian had worked at the Dry Dock when they were kids, and his hands showed evidence of the hard work he did. She loved his hands, so warm and strong. She loved it when he touched her, he could be so gentle but always firm. She didn't know how she would get through this, she swallowed thickly, her throat dry.

"Babe, you're scaring me." Ian's voice was barely above a whisper. He was more than scared. He was terrified of what he was sure was going to be disastrous.

"Ian," she met his eyes, trying to gather strength from him. "I..." she cleared her throat. "I've been thinking a lot the past little while and I think it's time I need to let you go. I'm not what you need. I distract you from your family, from the rest of your life, and it's not fair." She was shaking so badly that she didn't know how she managed to not slide out of her seat. "Today will be our last day together. We can't see each other anymore."

Ian pulled his hand out of her hold. He felt hot yet cold at the same time, he couldn't believe what he was hearing. It must be the ringing in his ears that made him not understand her words. He ran his hands through his hair in disbelief, not knowing what to say to her.

“What. The. Fuck.” He just spent 48 hours with her, 48 of the most perfect hours he’s ever had and now she was saying it was over? He didn’t understand.

“Please don’t do that, I need you to listen to me.”

“Listen to you? You’re not making any sense. What the fuck do you mean, let me go?” He couldn’t sit there with her. He got up from the sofa and went over to the balcony. The view that usually soothed him did nothing for him at this moment.

“If you’ll let me explain...” she started to say but was interrupted.

“You’d better start then because I’d really like to hear this.”His voice was uncharacteristically harsh, not that she could blame him; she could have eased into it.“This ought to be good.”

"I love you so much-" she tried to reach out to him, but he shrugged her off.

“Pfft”

“Don’t do that, don’t ever doubt the way I feel about you after everything we’ve been through, you know I love you.”

He didn't say anything. An hour ago, he would have agreed, but now she was talking about leaving him. You don't leave people you love for no good reason.

“Ian, please look at me.” She stood behind him, her hands flat on his back, he was rigid with tension.

“You keep telling me ‘soon’, you’ll come and see me soon and ‘someday, when we’re together’. We’re out of ‘soon’ and ‘someday’, Ian. We’re out of time.” Her voice trembled as she rested her forehead on his back, “God, I love you so much, I always have. I hope you know how much. I hope that you were always able to feel it. I tried so hard to make sure you never doubted it. I hope you’ll always remember for the rest of your life that I loved you more than anything. I would do anything for you.”

She swallowed back a sob, and her chest felt like it was breaking open. She could swear she actually felt the bones crack. She wrapped her arms around herself to keep the hurt inside.

Ian slowly turned around. His face was stony, Ian could do cold like nobody she had ever known. He offered no comfort, he was too angry, too hurt.

“Why then, babe? This doesn’t make any sense, if you love me then why are you doing this? I give you as much as I can. Am I not doing enough? Am I not paying attention to you enough? Not fucking you enough?”

“Don’t be like that. It has nothing to do with any

of those things.”

“Then why?” he shouted, making Essie cringe. “Jesus Christ, Essie. Tell me what’s going on. What’s the problem?” He gripped his hair in his hands, wanting to rip the strands out of his head.

"I'm out of time." She said again, "there won’t be a someday for us. We’ve wasted our whole lives dreaming about what could be and regretting that things weren’t different. It’s so sad, Ian; I’m so sad that we wasted so much time. I’m so sorry it’s going to end like this, we deserve better. I hope that someday, you can forgive me and you’ll remember the time we spent loving each other instead of this.”

Ian made his way to the closest chair and lowered his body to the seat, leaning his elbows on his knees, his hands hanging between his outstretched legs, deflated. He couldn’t believe what he was hearing. She had never even so much as hinted that she was unhappy.

“What does any of that even mean, Es?” Exhaustion flowed over him. “Are you punishing me for not being what you wanted?”

Essie felt sick, he looked so lost. She knew Ian was hurting and she hated that she was going to hurt him even more. She wished things could be different, but she had issued an ultimatum once before and it didn’t work out well, so she promised that she would never do it again. She hadn’t either. She had kept her word. She didn't push him for more than he could give. She didn't make demands on him, she accepted his boundaries and limits. He made it clear that while he loved her, he wasn't in a position to fight for her. She had learned to accept it and he would have to learn to accept this. She followed him to the chair he was sitting in and lowered herself to her knees in front of him, placing her hands on his thighs. She could feel the muscles jump under the thick denim.

"Ian, please look at me." She asked him again.

Something in her tone tugged at him. He raised his head. Her eyes, her gorgeous blue eyes were staring back at him, tears shimmering before spilling elegantly down her cheeks. He couldn't take her tears, he never could. It killed him when she cried. She knew this, always hiding them from him but she didn't have it in her today. Instead, she let them fall. He brushed them away with the pads of his thumbs, murmuring to her not to cry.

"I'm out of time because I'm sick," she said so quietly he almost missed the words. His hand stilled, the shock of what she just said slammed into him like a freight train. His ears were ringing, his chest felt like it was being squeezed and his guts ripped open. He was sure the room tilted. Was he having a heart attack? A stroke? Nausea rolled through his stomach. He thought of all of the times she asked to see him and he refused, all of the times he couldn't be bothered to tell her he loved her because he thought she already knew. He instantly remembered every missed opportunity to see her because he thought they would have more time. He knew every single time he made some lame excuse and she accepted it.

"What does that mean?" He asked her. He could feel the sting of tears, the bitter taste at the back of his throat, he tried to swallow past it.

“You’ve seen the bruises, you’ve noticed the weakness in my hands and legs, the slurred speech. You’ve mentioned the confusion, the stumbling and lack of coordination. You send me to the spa because you think I’m tired and I need the pampering. I’m not tired sweetheart. I’m dying. I have ALS.”

Ian knew what that was. Lou Gehrig’s disease. He was dumbfounded. “How long have you known?”

“Two and a half years.”

Ian stared at her. Two-and-a-half years. She’s known for two-and-a-half years. “Why didn’t you tell me?”

"At first, I didn't know how to. Later, I didn't want to burden you with it, and there's nothing you can do. I didn’t want to worry you. I wanted us to have as many good days as we could. I wanted this perfect two days with you so that after I’m gone, you would have these memories.” She reached out to take his hand, lacing her fingers through his to stop the shaking.

"I don't understand." He said bleakly. "How could you not tell me?"

Essie felt horrible that she was causing him pain. "It wouldn't have changed anything. There was nothing you could do. There's nothing anyone could do."

"I could have been there for you."

"No, sweetheart, you couldn't." She shook her head, closing her eyes to the pain in his. "You can't be. You never could. It's a nice thought, but realistically, you can't be there for me. I had to learn to accept that a long time ago, just like you're going to have to accept this. Just promise me that you'll never forget how much I love you, even after I'm gone. I hope you know that I have never regretted one single second of the time we spent together."

She opened her eyes and he saw it. The love she talked about was there in all of its brilliance. It broke open, not like a crack, but more like the walls falling down and he could see the light. It warmed him but made him sad. He didn't deserve it. He couldn't give her the life she should have had. He constantly disappointed her and always took her for granted. He was selfish. He knew that no matter what, she was always there for him, but he didn't do that for her. He was too stubborn to let his guard down, to try to give her a little bit of what she so freely offered to him. He was a coward, and now they were out of time. He would never be able to make it up to her. He would never be able to show her exactly how much he loved her. The pain in his chest grew. It was unbearable. He tugged her hand to bring her upon to his lap. He held her tight against his chest, so tight he could feel her heartbeat. He felt her breath as she sighed against his neck.

"I love you," she said softly.

"Hey, look at me, Es." Essie raised her head. She looked into the face of the man she had loved for her entire adult life. She wished they had more time, she wasn't done loving him. Ian brushed the hair away from her face.

"I'm sorry I wasn't a better man for you. I should have done things differently, but I always loved you. I'm always going to love you, you're my one." Ian eyes filled with tears, he tried hard to blink them away."I'm going to figure this out, we're not over."

Present Day

Ian got back in his truck, he grabbed a tissue from the box and wiped at the tears that had formed. Even after all this time, the wounds still felt fresh. He supposed they always would be. He started the engine and made his way from the Water Street condos to the City Market. He found a parking spot right across the street, *good timing* , he thought to himself. He fed the meter and made his way through the brick arch into the bustling market.

He stopped for a moment to appreciate the beauty of the oldest market in Canada. Built by shipbuilders in 1875, the ceiling looked like an inverted ship's keel. Everything you could possibly want was here. He and Essie had come up to stroll through the stalls on summer mornings every chance they could. They always stopped at the bakery before they left; Essie had a sweet tooth. He would stop there for a little something as soon as he got the flowers he came for.

The young girl working at the flower stall reminded him of Essie at 18: long blond hair, blue eyes, beautiful smile. She wrapped the daisies up carefully for him, asking if he would like a card to go with it. He shook his head no. She handed him the bouquet with a smile, offering him good wishes for the day. He thanked her and headed to the bakery.

Everything smelled so good, and though he wasn't in the mood for something sweet, but he got a breakfast sandwich and a coffee to go. He waited for just a few minutes for his turn to place his order. It was ready before he knew it. He paid for his order, including the tip, and went back to his truck. He lay the flowers on the seat next to him, put his coffee in the holder along with his breakfast and drove to the cemetery on Westmoreland Road. It was huge, but he knew exactly where he was going. There weren't too many visitors here today, which was a relief. He didn't want to share his grief with strangers.

Ian parked in the lane not far from Essie's grave. He sat still for a few minutes, letting the emotions flow over him. It was still so hard. She should be here with him, they should have grown old together. He took a deep breath, grabbed the flowers and with his breakfast from the bakery, made his way to where the love of his life rested.

As Essie's grave came into sight, he could see two figures standing nearby through the thick fog that had formed. He knew immediately who it was. He should have known that she wouldn't let him be alone today.

"Hey," he murmured as he came up behind them.

Alice turned around, a grin on her beautiful face. "Hi, Dad." She was two years older than Essie was when she died. She looked so much like her mother, same eyes, the shape of her face, same smile. Still, he could see parts of himself in her as well. She was the perfect combination of the both of them.

"What are you doing here?"

"It's her birthday, you didn't think I'd let you be alone, did you?" She hugged her father tightly. She pulled back after a moment and looked into his eyes, making sure he was doing ok.

"Hi, Gramp." Ian's grandson, Jack, stood close by.

"Hi, Jackie boy," He pulled his only grandchild into his arms. He was a good kid, smart as a whip.

"Where's the baby?"

Jack chuckled at his grandfather. Jack's little girl, Jenna was 6 but Ian always called her baby.

"She's in school, Gramp, she's looking forward to your date on Friday."

"Good." Ian had a special bond with Jenna. She was the brightest spot in his life. He tried to take her out for supper every Friday. "Come on then, let's get this visit going."

The family of three made their way around the huge tree to where Essie was buried. Ian stopped directly in front of the headstone, pleased to see that it was well maintained. He unwrapped the daisies and laid them on the green grass, brushing his fingers over the sun and stars that had been engraved on the marble.

<u>Stephanie Bennett</u>

<u>"Essie"</u>

<u>wife, mother, grandmother</u>

<u>1972-2024</u>

Ian had teased her about signing her cards and notes with just an "S", he started calling her "S," then "Essie" as a joke, but it stuck and he couldn't think of her any other way.

That day that she tried to end it between them, her 50th birthday, was the worst day of his life, but it was then that he realized he didn't want to be without her. He finally made a decision to leave his other relationship and be with Essie. They fought bitterly about it but in the end, he won. They got married two months later and he stayed by her side until the day she breathed her last breath.

"Are you ok, Dad?" Alice asked, gently stepping up beside him, Jack close behind.

"I loved her." Ian was often gruff but Alice knew that it was just his way. He had the biggest, softest heart of anyone she had ever known. She was angry with him for a few years once she found out that he was living with another woman for most of her life, but her mother made her see why it had to be like that. She eventually got over it and forgave them both. Alice loved her father and when her parents were together, it was clear to everyone that they only had eyes for each other.

"I know you did. She knew it, too," Alice assured him. She put her arm around her father's waist. "She would talk about you when I was a little girl, telling me about this grand love you had for each other – how she fell in love with the boy with the most beautiful green eyes in the world. She made it sound like a fairy tale."

Ian laughed. "That sounds like her. Her head was always in the clouds. She was completely ridiculous."

He shook his head, the acute pain in his chest making him miss her so much more. He kissed his daughter's forehead, telling her he loved her. He turned to his grandson, hugged him goodbye, reminding him to drop Jenna off Friday evening. He was just getting to his truck when the sky opened up. He looked up at the clouds, smiling to himself. Essie got him in the rain again.

Amanda Evans

The Polite Neighbour

A red drop of blood fell like a ruby meteor, crashing onto the patch of dirt, mingling with the blood of the rest of the family. Rowan's old matronly hand wrapped around the youth's wrist, massaging it out. Roland was the youngest grandchild of the Faithful. A throwback, he was a mirror image of his great- great- grandfather and Rowan hoped it was a good sign. Tonight was his first bloodletting; they would know soon.

When the small pinprick ceased to give more blood, she finally released him. He scuttled back to his mother, tears in his enormous eyes. The old woman's hand reached for the yew staff that was a relic of the old world, careful to avoid hitting the mushrooms that ringed the plot. She started mixing their blood with the earth of the old world and the dirt of Saint John. The newer dirt was resistant to the magic, but the older dirt folded over the blood and drank it deeply.

The woman started speaking, her words pouring forth with all the will - and the little magic - that she possessed pressed into them. They had the strange cadence of the Gaelic language. The rest of the family joined in, some unsure of themselves while others had a fluency with the old tongue. The ancient earth gave off a soft, sunny scent and the mushrooms had a slight glow, which was a new development in the past couple of ceremonies. The newer earth, however, still seemed lifeless. Salt permeated the air this close to the ocean, killing the magic, and even a hundred years of being inside a building had not done much to reduce the effect of the generations of salt that had splayed across the earth as it slept on the shoreline before the first man arrived here.

The intensity of the ritual made it hard to concentrate on anything else, but some part of her noticed the faint ringing of bells and the sound of laughter that shouldn't be. It wasn't her alone noticing the strange new sensations; all around her were the looks of wonder on her families' faces. She continued the chant; this was the most important of the year's rituals. The earth was waking, and they needed to call the magic to it. When the last syllable finished, the feeling that had built up popped audibly, like a thick-skinned soap bubble rupturing.

The ceremony completed, the room started waking. People blinked, others yawned or stretched, and as a pack they started to make their way towards the door. They headed into the yard, towards the patio and food. Habit had taught them that this was their next step, except for Roland. The youngster toddled sleepily towards the mushroom ring. "Mamma, look! The dirt is darker."

Margaret grabbed her son's arm, stopping him before he could get himself in trouble, but her eyes, as well as Rowan's, were on the dark, rich pile of loam.

The sun had set and the darkness was fully flung across the sky before everyone had left except for Rowan and the young Jennifer. Estranged from her family and their willful ways, she was now a ward and helper for the Carasoine family matron.

"Do you need anything, Ma'am?" Jennifer asked politely.

"My mead," Rowan wrinkled her nose, making a funny face for the youth, but the amusement never reached the old woman's eyes.

"Right away," Jennifer stated, and darted from the room. At 14 she was a lovely thing, devoted to the old ways as well. If she had even a lick of magic in her, she would have made a great Matron when Rowan's own time came to an end. She sighed deeply. So few branches of the family had stayed loyal to their legacy, and it felt like more were being sheered away every year of her watch. She made her way around the parlour. It was a small room, one she only used for reflection. The walls were done in polished wood and the beams in a darker lacquered wood. The rugs and the curtain on the small round window were various shades of green, as was the chair she would sink into. On each side of the chair was a wide, stone-gray table. It was a room that was reserved as a reminder of the magic of the old world, and regretfully, it was not often used nowadays.

Shortly after Rowan seated herself, Jennifer opened the door without knocking. She carried a small tray with a deep, heavy handled mug and an oddly shaped decanter of the honey-sweet brew, "Your mead. I don't know why you drink it," she wrinkled her nose.

It had an earthy, hoppy scent that was laced heavily with the sweetness of honey and left a clinging feeling in the back of the throat before it was even tasted.

"Magic, my dear," Rowan answered as she had for the past two and a half years, and like the previous times she was asked, she didn't elaborate. "Please set it down, I'll be here until after you've gone to sleep. Have a good night child," she dismissed the girl.

She felt some sadness at the life the child was leading. She had few friends, hurrying home from school as she did most days. But Rowan was too old and set in her ways to allow children to run amok in the house. During the summer she'd let the child have a full run of the fenced-in yard so long as they stayed away from the bay. She may even see about getting a pool for them.

"Have a good night," Jennifer said politely before she left the room and closed the door.

The bottle on the tray had not yet started to drip with condensation, but it had become opaque under the haze. It was oddly shaped, like a gourd, and looked like the image from the old books. It was old, much older than the young girl. Charles, Rowan's husband, had bought it for her shortly after they had been wed, and like the marriage, the brew and the memories were bittersweet, with emphasis on the sweet. Rowan let out a raspberry with her pursed lips. She hated the taste of the too-sweet liquor. In her youth she'd preferred vodka and scotch but as heavy and teeth-rotting as it was, it was the drink of the druids, so it was what she had on ritual nights. She poured herself a glass, the amber liquid close to overflowing. Steeling herself, she drank deeply, but still winced as the sickly sweet taste hit. It was a relief when the mead's power overtook her senses.

She let the events of the day and the ritual roll through her mind. The magic that they had all experienced today was more than just the accumulation of the family's power. It was strong, it had made the earth turn and the air sing, and it bound the family tightly together. She smiled, a look that still made her look decades younger than she was. The magic - it was the boy. The sunny scent and the glowing ring started when Margaret became pregnant with the child. She could barely hold in the excitement, she wanted to tell everyone, to show them, remind them of what they could be, but with a pessimist's pragmatism, she stopped herself before she'd even roused from the chair. She would wait until the next ritual and see how things went before telling anyone of what was going to become of them.

The mead held her, wrapping its strong alcoholic arms around her, dragging her into the living dream that comes from drinking. Sinking deeper into the chair, she let whatever was to come, come. The tolerances one has in youth doesn't last until one was almost 70, even with the magic in her blood to stave off most of the ravages of age. Her eyes closed and her head rocked back against the leaf green pillow.

The magic in the old lands was starting to fail. The druids could feel it, even the common man could feel it. The Good Neighbour was making fewer and fewer sojourns into this world because of the human's liberal use of iron, the killing metal, and the magic was fading because of it. There were only a dozen or so places in all the isles that they could still cross that were not polluted with doubt, filth, and iron. A great convocation of druids was called - the greatest that was remembered, even in myth, since the days of Emrys. The need to restore the magic across the world overrode the druids' need to stay away from mankind and their flow of history. A dozen sets of the druids were tasked with this job. They were to take earth from the sacred circles along with the blessed mushrooms and they were to create magic circles wherever they could. It was tasked to them and their descendants through perpetuity until they restored the magic.

Regar and Merwyn were selected to go west, and that travel brought them to the newly landed . The land here was as dead of magic as any they had ever seen, the salty brine killing the magic before it could be birthed. The two druids argued mightily about moving beyond the coast, somewhere that the magic would flourish easier, but Merwyn was unwilling to relent. If the magic and their descendants could thrive here, the magic would be safe and could be transferred anywhere in the world.

The ages washed past, ancestor after ancestor building on to this home and this cave of magic. The red stone walls were washed in all the magic the druids and their descendants could impart. The ceremonies and rituals flowed with no changes and no improvements. The faith of the family faded. Everything was fading, and then tonight's ritual...

Rowan woke from the dream, pride and stiffness at war within her. She stood, looking at her watch: 5:45 in the morning. She moved stiffly towards the door, wincing at each step as she started feeling her legs. The door opened quietly, and she turned off the lights. It was dark in the hall, but she'd known these halls all of her life and she could navigate them blindfolded. She stifled a groan as she thought of how tiring the trip to the market was going to be.

When she woke at 11:30 AM, the house was quiet, and Jennifer was in school. Rowan showered and dressed quickly in her out-to-town suit and walked the dozen blocks towards the market. She never really understood why her ancestors had chosen the spot that they had, but in her opinion, it was a good one to make. She lived close to the water, though the smell sometimes made it a mixed blessing. The street was wider than most, and rumor had it that before her time, this was a street used by trolleys, first horse-drawn, then electric. The divide in the middle had trees and there was shade to keep it cool and beautiful during the warmer weather. She passed through the Loyalist Burial Grounds, stopping as she often did by the beaver fountain. She passed parallel to King's Square, past the DMV and the gap that used to house the Paramount Movie Theatre. At one time, it was the pride of the Paramount company, but as with most things in Saint John, it had fallen into disrepair. Then she was at the City Market; it was one of the few places that the city protected, and it would not be left to rot.

The market was a riot of sights, sounds. Rowan's eyes took in more than the stalls and the goods; her eyes also took in the people. They ebbed and flowed around her, seeing her as unworthy of their time, just an old woman blocking their path. She saw nothing in them worthy of the work of bringing magic back for nothing to make her family's sacrifice worth the time. She saw women in clothes too short, and men in clothes too informal; she saw piercings and tattoos and hair, the colours that no decent human should have, colours reserved for the Fae. There were so many people with their face down, looking at their phones and their distractions, not living life, not living to their potential, living instead as zombies to a technical overlord.

Changes. So many things had changed since her forefathers had landed. They were necessary, and it was a sadness that gripped her and often made her wonder if their life's work was still necessary. They had electricity, and TV, and even a computer. She watched movies that could make magic as flashy as any in the tales, but with less pain and condemnation than the Fae used. The maudlin feeling bogged at her, dragging her down. She paid with cash, a habit in itself that was becoming antiquated, and left. The park pulled at her; she needed the grass and the trees. Crossing the street, she entered the park laid out like a Union Jack; not many people remembered that geographical fact any longer. She found a bench free of homeless people to sit on and rest her weary bones and her shopping bag.

The sun was warm on her face. The sun was warm on her face. The pigeons cooed, and the ravens cawed, swarming around her. She let these sensations relieve the icy darkness of uncertainty that shaded her thoughts. Humanity always took from her what nature gave so easily and readily, without stinting - a sense of being, of purpose and relief.

"Hey, lady," a small boy said. "Have ye got n'e'thin' fer me?" His words were reminiscent of the homeland she had never been to.

Rowan was ready to chase away the impertinent child, but stopped. He wasn't a child. Small as a toddler, that was true, but he was a man, or man-like, actually. The small brown suit and the accent brought back the images from the books that came across the sea.

"I have naught here for ye," she told him with reverence, "but come by our home and I will make sure there is something left out for you and yours."

The small man creature tipped his hat and bowed low. "That will be much appreciated."

"Sir, may...may I have yer name?" she queried nervously, hands in her lap and eyes on him.

"Lady, if ye need to, ye ken call me Wormell," he told her and then he faded out of sight, a glamour; the earth here would not accept his magic. Rowan leaped to her feet and hustled along the concrete walkway, almost forgetting the bag of food she'd recently bought.

It was past lunch by the time she returned home; Jennifer had come and gone, the evidence of her being here stacked in the sink and crumbs on the counter. Rowan had no glower for the mess; she had seen one of the Good Neighbours. Her mind was awhirl with thoughts, memories of lore all but forgotten. Milk? Honey? Bread? Cookies? She wracked her mind, trying to remember what they liked. It was hard to guess, as she didn't know exactly what Fae she was dealing with. She guessed Brownie because of his coat, but he could have been anything.

With an exasperated huff, she decided on one of each. She put her groceries away and made up platters of food. Covering it with fine domes, she moved them out onto the veranda. It was cool enough that it wouldn't go bad too quickly. She put it close to the tree and took off back into the house.

When Jennifer came home, the honey, milk, and cookies were long gone; the dome held only the single sandwich. It could have been a cad. The wooden trellis and the mesh aluminum fence would do little to keep out anyone that wanted in, but Rowan knew it had been the Fae. She kept the secret close to her chest while she and her family ate and talked through the evening. She wanted to get her thoughts straight before she said a word.

The next morning Rowan awoke early, hope renewed in her soul. The house was clean. Much cleaner than they had left it the night before. Everything gleamed, even the yard was tidier than yesterday, and the spring flowers had grown higher.

“Definitely a Brownie,” her words were smug as she went about making her tea.

The brownie made himself known another twenty

or so times in the next six months, but he never again said a word to those that lived in the house. Perhaps he was afraid that there would be the death metal - iron - in the house, or perhaps they just simply weren't outside when he was. He never stayed long; he was just a flash through the glass and gone. He wasn't the only one of the Fae that showed themselves. -Sometimes there were little visions dancing in the fog as it rolled across the land so close to the water. They could have been the water sprites - undines, or sylphs - the Fae spirits of the air. This close, it really could be either. It didn't much matter as they were magical, beautiful beings that disappeared just as quickly as they appeared, leaving only a dance and a happy memory in their wake.

Every evening, either Jennifer or herself made sure to leave an offering. She had told Jennifer of the discovery of a lesser Fae, and that the magic was returning. No one else, not even those that lived within the walls took notice of the gifts that the brownie left. Most often it just cleaned the house to a sparkle or worked in the yard, but sometimes he brought material gifts: tiny gifts of great value and workmanship. Jennifer now wore a beautiful rose quartz heart on a golden chain, a gift found under the tray early into the second month of the arrangement, and on Rowan's desk there was a small tree, no bigger than the palm of her hand with a trunk of tiger's eye, leaves of green agate, and tiny chips of garnet for the apples. The look of the trunk and its branches mimicked the apple tree in the backyard.

Rowan had never in her life felt happier or closer to their goal, and once this filial obligation was complete, they would be free. It wasn't something that Rowan had expected to have happened during her lifetime. Since Regar and Merwyn, there was doubt that anyone would ever be able to complete the ceremony, until Roland.

"Mother," Margaret greeted, stepping into the dayroom. In most houses it would be an office, a library, or a living room, but the old woman was stuck in the past, in the English past at that, and this room lacked the light to be a solarium but it still deserved a grander name than 'office'.

"Margaret," Rowan acknowledged with a nod as she finished the last column of numbers in her puzzle and put the pen down to give her daughter her full attention. "To what do I owe the pleasure?"

Margaret walked into the room, closing the door behind her; although Jennifer was part of the family, and discrete, Margaret wanted this matter kept to themselves. She crossed the room. Grabbing a chair and pulling it close to her mother, she sat before speaking. "I want you to stop these ceremonies," she said softly, taking her mother's hand.

"Stop them, whatever for? They're working," Rowan replied, sitting up straighter, confused.

"No, Mother, they're not." Margaret shook her head. "You want them to work, so you think they are. You're convincing yourself they are," she squeezed her mother's hand affectionately, the smile offering reassurance.

Rowan pulled her hand back from her daughter's warm grip, her eyes showing the wound. "But Roland's blood is working. He has the power that we've been searching for for generations!" she countered and pushed herself from the chair, taking a couple of steps as her voice rose in pitch.

Margaret fought to keep her tone mild, to not get carried away and start ranting and raving like her mother. "Mom. It's dirt. That's all it is, that's all it has ever been," she said it. It was a harsh truth that she and her siblings had discussed a lot over coffee over the last couple of months. "I'm not going to take part in your ceremony anymore."

"I don't need you," Rowan hissed, her face starting to glow red, a dreadful color against her green eyes and gray hair.

"I won't let Roland take part anymore either," Margaret added, something that she thought would have been obvious.

Those words slapped like ice against the old woman, her red face paling to linen white in a breath. "You can't stop him from taking part. He's the key!"

"And that belief is why he's not going to take part anymore," she told her mother, her defensive instincts kicking in. "If you insist on behaving like this, then you won't ever see your grandson again," Margaret told her. "I love you, mom, but this has gone on too long."

The old woman stumbled to her chair and sank down. "I don't understand? How can you turn your back on our legacy?" Her words were intense and her gaze searched for the evil in her daughter, as if by seeing where it hid, she could route it.

"It's a story, mom, that's it," she spoke slowly, shaking her head. She reached out and met her mother's searching hand.

"You couldn't feel the magic? When the earth was stirred?"

The younger woman looked down sheepishly, not wanting to lie to her mother. She had felt something, but it could have been anything - anticipation, or just getting caught up in the mood of the crowd. She didn't truly think it was magic. That look said more to her mother than all of her words.

"How long have you felt this way?" she asked softly, her free hand raising to caress her daughter's hair.

"For a while, a couple of years. Since Roland was born, maybe?" she answered without conviction.

There was a sadness building in her. She knew she was destroying something; she knew it was her relationship with her mother, but also feared it was her mother's soul. "Ethan feels the same way."

Rowan's lips drew down into a frown and the lines deepened in her face. She didn't care what Ethan felt. A threat to her family, he was a man who should know nothing of their ceremonies; his sole use was his part of the DNA that made Roland

"Just Ethan?" Rowan pressed.

"And Arthur, and Elizabeth," Margaret stated.

Rowan closed her eyes to keep the anger and disappointment deep under the veneer of sadness and acceptance. "Oh," she said. "I see."

"I'm sorry Mom, we didn't want to hurt you ... " her words trailed off.

"I understand." It was a heartbreaking sound, the words that came from her. "I think I would like to be alone for a while, if you don't mind, dear?"

Margaret's eyes darted around the room for a second, not sure what to do or say. Resentful that she was the only one of her siblings with the backbone to do this; she had never wanted to hurt her mother.

"Sure, Mom." She stood and then leaned down to kiss the aged cheek. "Call me if you need anything?"

Rowan nodded, but didn't say anything, her mind working so furiously she barely even noticed anything was said at all. The day wore on as Rowan sat alone in her room, trying to figure out how to move on. She was close, so very close, to finally finishing what her great ancestors had started. Even if they wouldn't admit it, everyone had felt the magic.

"Rowan?" Jennifer's voice came through the tiny gap she'd opened in the doorway.

"What do you want, Jennifer?" Rowan asked, her face turning towards the youngster. She was probably the prettiest little thing the family has produced in generations.

"There is a gentleman here to see you," she said nervously, nudging the door open a little wider.

"I don't want to speak with him right now. Tell him to call back later." She spoke harshly to the woman-child. Rowan regretted her tone before the words had all tumbled out of her mouth, but she didn't have the patience for some solicitor to come to call.

"I think not!" a tall gentleman stated with a false anger in his voice. He pushed past the girl, causing her to shiver, throwing the door open wide.

Rowan's jaw dropped when she took him in. He was one of the high Fae, a Seelie or an Unseelie. She couldn't tell his court at a glance but she could tell that he was a Faerie far more powerful and deadly than the little Sylphs, Gnomes, and Undines that had visited her. “Sir... Majesty...” Her words dried up.

The man smirked. He was taller and more slender than any man she'd ever seen; his hair was long and straight and if it wasn't for the old-fashioned clothes he wore, she would be hard pressed to tell if he was a man at all, so androgynous was his form.

Jennifer's eyes darted between the two in the room. She'd lived here a long time and had yet to see the druidic matron be cowed by anyone. “Ma'am?” she asked, her own voice catching on the feeling in the air. Danger lurked in this man’s wake.

"That's okay, Jennifer, it's alright. I want to speak with him. Tea?" she asked her guest in the same breath.

"Finally, someone that knows the lost arts of civility. Yes. Lots of sugar, and some scones or sweets of some kind or other," he demanded.

"Ma'am?" Jennifer asked.

"Please, child, do as he asks."

"Yes, ma'am," she said and moved away from the doorway as quickly as her young and lithe form could get her out of sight.

"Perhaps you should shut the door?" Rowan

suggested when the girl was gone, amusement in her eyes. "I would do it myself, but I've grown old, and even an old lady knows that the Good Neighbour would not be harmed in this house."

He bowed low, a courtly gesture, but there was humor in his eyes. Without the child to impress, they had resumed their reptilian appearance with slits for pupils. "Very well," he agreed and shut the door. "You are correct, this house alone lacks the disgusting iron that seems necessary to keep this world upright. A druid's bloodline indeed."

"So you know of us?" Rowan asked after the door closed and the man before her had moved to make himself comfortable on the seat that her traitorous child had so recently graced.

"No, not so much, but we felt the stirring of the blood on the earth. Magic will ignite there soon." He told her, giving promise to that which she had felt during the ceremony. He validated everything.

"Will ignite?" she asked him. "How are you here if it hasn't ignited yet?"

"I suppose that I should introduce myself." He stood again and swept into a bow, taking her old hand and kissing the back of it in a gesture as natural to him as it was foreign to those from this land. "I am Zeletra, half-breed."

"Half-breed?" she asked, looking him over. She

took in the gold-white hair, long and bound back, emerald green eyes, elongated ears; his whole being was as delicate as if spun by a master.

"Three-quarters-breed if we must be so accurate." He smiled at the words. "I have the access to the magic in spades, but I also have the..." he coughed delicately, "aversion to the death metal." His smile was grand, a beautiful look if you ignored the sharpness of teeth and the threat they hid.

"How can I help you?" she asked, sitting up straighter. Along with the ceremonies and the bloodlines, she had been taught from youth about how to broker deals with the devils of underhill so that she would not lose her soul in the exchange.

"First, I think we should have the tea your delightful niece is struggling to bring to us, then we can speak about why I have chosen to call on you."

He opened the door before she could knock. She stumbled, but not enough for the hot tea to slosh. Her cheeks were tinted pink. "Thank you," she mumbled and hurried into the room, setting the tray on the desk. "Did you need any help?" she asked, but her eyes darted to the man that scared her.

"No dear, we're fine, you can go," she said, to the great relief of the girl.

The two adults said nothing as the child scampered out of the room, closing the door behind her. "I would have liked to have kept her as a treat," Zeletra pouted, taking a Girl Guide cookie off the tray. Rowan shot him a scathing glare that cheered him up considerably.

"Now, shall we continue the conversation we were about to have?" she asked, turning away from him to make her tea. Sweetened with honey and nothing else, as tea was meant to be. The cubes of sugar were on the tray for his sake.

"I want the child," he stated directly - an action uncommon to his mixed heritage.

"Jennifer is not a treat," Rowan countered with no mirth.

"Not Jennifer, the boy." The change of subject confused the older woman, and she looked at him with eyes that reflected it. "The boy with the magic," he clarified.

Understanding flooded her face. "Roland? Why?" she asked and then cursed silently at herself for providing him with a knowledge of the child's name for free.

"He has old magic. We want him to bring that magic back to those of the faith." She could tell that he was speaking the truth. He couldn't lie, none of his kind could, but that didn't mean they were trustworthy.

"So nothing major, then?" she asked with a smirk.

He glared at her and her mockery. The Good Neighbour mocked, humanity trembled; that was the way of things. Her smirk faded. "I don't know that either of us will have access to the young lad," she told him in seriousness. "His mother was here earlier and said that she wouldn't allow him to take part in any more ceremonies."

The Fae's eyebrow arched up higher. "You are her mother, are you not? Your word is law in this family, is it not?"

"Old people are just old now, not elders," she informed him, her shoulders slumping forward. Her age seemed even greater than the significant years she had lived. "As the magic of your people faded, so did the rule of the elders on earth," she sighed.

He gave back a wicked look. "Seems we have much in common, and much that we must change." She nodded, agreeing with him with all of her heart and belief. "What must be done to get this child back in our hands? A changeling perhaps?"

"That wouldn't work. She is likely to visit, and that would be a difficult thing to explain." She pursed her lips, at a loss of what could be done that would give her unrestricted access to the child without harm to the parents.

"Then we must be rid of the parents," he stated simply.

"You may not hurt them. My daughter has been misled by the man-child of the new God, but she is still my child."

Power flared around him, making the room feel like it was trembling. “You are in no position to barter; you have nothing to offer, and no control over your kin," he told her. "But I will give my word that I will not hurt them, or see them in harm’s way. I will just remove them from the picture for a time."

She breathed a sigh of relief that he added the additional promises. He was right; she had nothing to barter with and no way to keep anyone safe. "I will raise the child to believe in our ways as his parents did not," she promised. "I will help you and your...” She paused; it wasn't just his cause, it's what her family had been trying to accomplish for generations. “Our cause any way that I can.”

“Good,” he stated, tipping back his cup. His throat moved to allow him to swallow. “Then I will come to visit you again when I am done.”

“What do you plan to do to them?” she asked nervously. Even with his promise, he had left himself a vast canyon of wiggle room.

“For your own sake, I am not going to tell you that.” He placed the cup on the tray and stood. Then he was gone before she could think of a way to make him tell her. With him gone, she was left to think of the strangeness of the Fae. Everything about them was different: the way they thought, the way they acted, even how they looked. After seeing Zeletra, really seeing him, she didn't know how she could have ever thought he was human- androgynous or not. He was more lithe than anyone she had ever seen, more delicate, more ethereal, and he carried power around him like a cloak. The ears and eyes he could glamour, but he was not human or alien. He was what he was, and it showed.

The ceremony passed, without Roland and that branch of the family, and without Rowan or Jennifer sharing what they knew. Two and a half months passed where nothing happened - no word from the Good Neighbour or from Margaret. Rowan began to worry that her time would pass before the Fae made his move.

"Ma'am," Jennifer said softly, knocking on the door to the parlor, where the old matron found herself more often than not.

"Yes?" she called out, and the door opened, revealing her young ward.

"There are some people here to see you." There was anxiety showing on the child. "The police, and they have Roland with them."

Rowan sat up straight. "Bring them in, please," the girl turned and hurried down the hallway again. Now that she was listening, Rowan could hear how fast she was moving. She couldn't hear the words that passed between, but there were a lot of feet coming back towards her.

She stood to greet them as the door opened. Two police officers, a mostly human looking Zeletra, and Roland filed into the room. There was no blood and nothing to indicate that anything bad had happened, but the party was too somber and the air they brought with them was wrong. Tears started to well up. They leaked down her cheeks and she sank, her knees weak.

"Mrs. Carisoine?" the bigger man in the front asked.

"Yes?" she whispered, but it felt like a wail to her own ears.

"We would like to speak with you for a few minutes if you don't mind." It wasn't a question. He made it sound as sympathetic as he could while still being matter-of-fact.

"Of course, what can I do for you?" she asked, her voice low and shaking.

"Do you know this child?" he asked indicating needlessly to Roland who was pale as a ghost and just as quiet.

"Of course! He’s my grandson, Roland Carlisle," she looked at all the men again slowly. "What's this about?"

"I have some questions about the boy's parents," the main speaker said; his partner shifted behind him. He was a small man, cleanly shaved and unattractive looking.

"Jennifer, can you take Roland out to the kitchen, get him a snack, and keep him company?" Even though it was phrased as a question, there was no mistaking it for a demand.

"Gentlemen, would you like something to drink? A snack?" The men shook their head no as Jennifer collected up the small boy and left the room.

The small sounds of children murmuring was all they could hear as the two of them made their way down the hall. Zeletra closed the door when they could hear nothing.

"What's this all about?" Rowan asked, a little stronger now that the children were gone.

The speaker shifted his feet. "Mrs. Carisoine, my partner, Officer Elliot, and I were called out to Hardings' Point Campgrounds earlier today when this gentleman," he vaguely indicated towards Zeletra, "Mr. Levesque-"

"Zachery Levesque, pleasure to meet you," Zeletra interrupted, stepping forward to shake Rowan's hand. His was cold to the touch and the glamour was fading, most likely from traveling by car.

"I'd return the niceties, but I don't think this is a time for them," she said still shaken.

The officer gave the Fae a look that spoke volumes about the small-man complex that he was sporting and how no one should interrupt his show. "Mr. Levesque called the police when he saw the bo... Roland wandering around seemingly alone at the campground over the course of the afternoon." A sob rose to her throat. "We searched the campgrounds and couldn't find any sign of them." He paused to give her time to process the words. Years on the job made tears powerless against him. It was a part of the reason he was on his third marriage.

"A... are they... you couldn't ... find..." Her words trailed off weak.

"We could find no sign of them. The campground has you listed as an emergency contact," he continued but her head was whirling.

For the next three quarters of an hour the police asked questions and Rowan answered to the best of her ability, but the words were not sinking in as they should. When she was asked later she could remember only one out of dozens of questions. The entire time Zeletra-cum-Zachery just stood in the background, his glamour staying fixed. Knowing him for what he was, the glamour did not work on her and she could see his cold eyes watching her. The only thing that she knew from their conversation was that Roland was going to be her ward unless his parents came back and were deemed fit to take custody of him again, or they could find any legal documentation giving instruction on the care of the child.

When it was over, Rowan rose from her seat and showed them out, forgetting that Zeletra had not accompanied them. She returned in a fog to the room to mull the situation over, and to have her tears, for what she had done to the child before she went to see him. Rowan knew he was in good hands with Jennifer, and Rowan had to stay strong for him; she couldn't break down in front of the children.

"So, it would seem that the child is in your care." The words seemed to come from the walls themselves. Rowan muffled her scream and the wall by the door rippled as the glamour dropped and Zeletra stepped forward. The vague mask of humanness sloughed away and he stood in his full beautifully terrifying half-blood visage.

"So it would seem," she said with a calmness that she didn't feel as she sunk into her chair. "You didn't hurt them."

The look that crossed his face could chill blood. "I gave you my word, did I not?" She nodded. "Then they were not hurt, nor are they in harm's way. They will be able to find their way back eventually."

"Way back?" she asked. "Eventually?" Worry for

her daughter was stronger than her fear.

“They are underhill and you know the lore as well as any that walk the green earth and better than those that tread only the dead gray stuff,” he stated impatiently, telling her that he was responsible for their disappearance. He'd led them to Faery. "To them but a few hours would have passed, but here, a couple of years, a decade, who knows?" he shrugged.

She nodded. She couldn't speak, couldn't even think properly. In eons past the Fae would have just stolen them or Roland away and no one would have been able to stop him. At best Zeletra would have left a changeling in their stead, but the days for that were gone; now they were just deadbeat parents. At some point, they would come back. By the time they did, it would take them years to prove themselves fit to take Roland back and by then he'd be of an age to make his own decisions. "Thank you," she said with a wash of relief, not for anything that he'd done, but for what he had not done.

"Well, if everything is taken care of, I'll see myself out, but I will be back to check on him," he advised and moved to open the door.

"You're coming to check on him?" Rowan asked. Concerned, she leaned forward and gave away much more than she intended to.

"Of course,” he stated, looking confused. “I need

the blood of that druid to bring back the magic of my people. Besides, I live close by, and I am, above all, a polite neighbour."

Maryam Syed

Maryam is originally from Pakistan, living in Saint John, New Brunswick. For as long as she can remember, she has always had several stories in her head, waiting to spill out on paper and weave their narrative. Her stories feature strong characters who overcome unprecedented struggles and challenges. As an immigrant, her writing voice holds a unique perspective that comes from being on the outside, looking in.

When the tanks roll in

The columns of men will march

You'll see

Tall buildings will fall

And the ghosts of broken children will play

in the jungle gym of concrete

You'll see

The sky will turn grey and the rain of blood will fall

It will impound the sins of men

You'll see

When fingers dig through the earth looking for fingers smaller still

The anguish of the searcher will rip through the earth

You'll see

The hearts of men will not melt

The hearts of men will not melt

You'll see.

Almond Eyes

The wind was strong in this city. It carried the smell of decaying leaves. It tugged on the scarf around Neelo's head, hair escaping from the loosened edges and brushing against her cheeks. It lifted a corner of Zafar's suit and carelessly released it. Where they came from, the wind had turned. It carried gunpowder and loss.

Dark clouds gathered behind three identical houses rubbing shoulders with each other, anchored in silent comradery. Their new home was the blue one on the right. A wooden house with a red door.

Does a wooden house crumble like concrete, Neelo thought, or does it fall in sharp shards that cut, not bury? Does it char or burn, and do the acrid fumes still crawl down the back of your throat? Did it silence screams? The screams of a child... Zafar stood by her elbow, at the periphery of her sight. Did he have the same thoughts?

They travelled without luggage. Everything they had, they wore. Neelo's wrists were laden with gold bangles she wore last on her wedding day with Zafar. The morning they left, Ammi, her mother, slid the bangles on her wrist one by one. Each bangle added to the weight of the ones already on her wrist, all of them hanging heavy. Ammi had knelt on her knees when she did this. The red velvet box that harboured

Neelo's jewellery was open by her side on the bed. It was empty at the end, its contents resting around Neelo's neck and wrists, its gaping mouth dark. Neelo watched the purple veins snaking like tributaries across Ammi's eyelids and the crow's feet at the corners of her eyes that deepened every time she blinked.

Through their journey in the crush of bodies in a cargo aircraft, the cold bangles grew warm and hung heavier. Neelo touched them when they climbed the ramp and felt her connection with Ammi.

Inside the blue house with the red door, a small foyer and carpeted stairs led to the apartment on the first floor. Zafar climbed up ahead and Neelo followed behind, her fingertips lightly grazing the bannister, feeling the ridges in the worn wood. Zafar spoke to her, but the stained wallpaper absorbed the words. Up ahead, the sinking sun shone through the landing window, darkening his silhouette. Fusty carpets and damp corners. The dampness settled in behind her ears, the ache spread across the back of her head and deep into her temples. Was that the sound of a baby crying? The puckered white scar across the bottom of her belly tingled and twisted.

They had left at dawn when the shapes of their city melted into each other in shades of grey and dusk. It was quiet. The sky sat atop the earth like an oppressive dome. Bare trees pointed to the sky and no birds chirped, nature gave this city a wide berth. Fires that erupted often had left charred remnants. They walked with silent steps through decimated rubble, changing course often to reach the tarmac.

Earlier, under the awning of the sky, a fragmented selection of their family had stood in a subdued semicircle and bid them goodbye. The silence was crushing, their grief palpable. The street where they grew up was at the rim of the city and the war inched closer. Ammi stroked

Neelo's face with translucent hands, her papery fingers lightly scraping her skin. Neelo thought Ammi would dissolve and disappear right before her eyes. If she did and became one with the air, this war would spare her.

Abba, her father, was already dead. He was returning from the market with a plastic shopping bag full of ice lollies for Neelo, when he kneeled over and stopped breathing of a heart attack in a quiet alley. When he was found, the ice lollies had melted, forming a sticky orange puddle by his head. When as a child, Neelo imagined her parent's death, she imagined them old and withered and breathing their last in a bed surrounded by their grandchildren. Her children. Neelo was a mother, but if her child was no longer alive, did she remain a mother still? Was Ammi still a grandmother? Was her father, who died before his grandchild was born, a grandfather? Neelo had not known that her mother would die so she could live. That leaving this city meant Neelo was killing her. She would never see her again. This war would take her.

Neelo remembered Ammi on her wedding day. Ammi's face lit up, her laugh high and real. She flung a garland of roses around Zafar's neck and embraced him. She danced with the women of the family, her arms in the air, beckoning the sky and thanking God.

When Neelo moved back home to give birth to her baby, Ammi wiped the sweat from her brow and stood calm and stoic when the midwife urged them to rush to the hospital. Zafar had sped through snaking streets to the hospital on the other side of the city. Neelo's writhing head was in Ammi's lap, the shadows of bare trees on this night of the full moon shifted on her face. Ammi stroked Neelo's damp hair and bulging belly with trembling fingers not yet translucent.

She was born through an incision in Neelo's belly. They named her Quratulain and called her Annie. Her name meant coolness of the eyes. The scar from the incision bound Neelo to her daughter. It stretched and ached when Annie cried through the night. Years later, when the scar had healed and Annie was old enough to walk to school, it twisted every morning Annie left the house in her starched baby blue school uniform, the straps of her book bag weighing down slight shoulders, her slender fingers waving goodbye.

It was the night before Eid al-Fitr1. Annie was 10 and the impending war was still an uncomfortable distant rumour. Skirmishes erupted in parts of the country, separated from them by miles. It did not seem real. The chandraat bazaar2 erected in the centre of the city twinkled under fairy lights, teeming and thronging with families, licking dripping ice cream cones and eating deep fried pakoras wrapped in greasy squares of newspaper. Like every year since Annie was 4, Zafar brought Annie to the bazaar where she bought glass bangles from the churi-wala and had her palm painted with henna at the mehndi stall. Neelo stayed home, cooking a vat of sweet vermicelli for the family visiting their house the next day for Eid.

Annie held onto Zafar's hand, glass bangles the colour of the setting sun clinked on her slender wrist. She had chosen the bangles herself from the churi-wala at the bazaar, a chandraat tradition. Delicate henna patterns dried on the palm of her other hand. She held it out, palm facing the sky, careful not to smudge the drying henna.

The blinding blaze lit the centre of the bazaar first, the blast drowning the shrieks. The explosion knocked Zafar in the air and stole his consciousness. The last thing he remembered was Annie's small hand slipping from his palm and his fingers desperately grasping at air. Zafar's body survived. Why then did he feel like he had lost a limb?

Neelo dug for Annie for days. Searching for her sunset bangles and for the fresh henna on the palm of her hand. Her fingernails bloody, her hands lacerated, she never found her daughter's broken body.

Ammi had disappeared a little then, when washing Neelo's bloody hands in the white wash basin. She watched the blood dilute and swirl and disappear down the drain and a part of her disappeared with it. In the dark drain below, her anguish had gone to hide. She bandaged Neelo's hands and the lines on her face became deep crevices into which her tears pooled.

The living room was dark. It led to a bedroom on one side and opened to a small kitchen on the other. Red Formica kitchen counters were the colour of warm bricks that paved the vast veranda at home. Home.

The apartment was already furnished with mismatched pieces of furniture. There was loneliness in their incongruity. A brown sofa with faded arms, a table by the window and two wooden chairs, a bed that creaked into the night and an emptiness that echoed.

"We will be safe here, Neelo," Zafar said.

He stood in the middle of the living room,

observing the apartment with inherent optimism. His earnestness was magnified behind thick spectacles. The safari suit he wore was wrinkled from their journey across the ocean. It once belonged to his father.

Zafar was reaching out in his desperate simplicity. He was trying to reassure her. Neelo nodded, her lips placid. A lump swelled in her heart and painfully rose to her throat. We will be safe, Zafar, but what of those we left behind?

A group called the Refugee Welcome Association had stocked their fridge and their closets. A handwritten note on the fridge detailed important phone numbers. The note was held in place with a lone refrigerator magnet shaped like a watermelon.

There was a stack of glossy papers on the kitchen counter, including a map folded into a tight square that held within itself a shrunken rendition of the foggy city that stretched out on all sides of this apartment. The local mosque and the offices of the Refugee Welcome Association had hasty circles around them.

As Zafar rifled through the papers, Neelo stared out the window at the maple tree in their backyard, its distinctive leaves fiery shades of red and orange. They fell to the grass below, forming a circular carpet.

She would spend many mornings at this window in the days and weeks to come. Nursing a cup of tea, her eyes staring out the window would not see the tree that shed its leaves, but instead would play a reel from the past in a relentless loop. When she came to and sipped from the cup still full, it would be cold.

Armed with typed copies of his resume within a file folder, Zafar left the next morning to search for work in this city by the sea where the air was salt and the seagulls screeched. Fog curled around polished shoes and faded creases. The yellow pages in the folder curled at the edges, the grey letters crawled, forming sentences in broken English, pregnant with loss.

"Owner, family ceramic manufacture and sale business, Peshawar Pottery"

Zafar was born in opulence. But when the war touched his city, the gold coffers of his family turned to lead. He was the one who found his father in the remnants of their factory; the bullet had pierced his throat, the dark gun lay on the floor by his limp hand. By then, Zafar was not a stranger to loss.

When his father's remaining brother, who Zafar called Chacha, pooled the family wealth together for him and Neelo to escape, at first he said no. His family was his strength, his coven. He had told Neelo that night when they lay in bed, his fingers laced through hers, an arm folded under his head, the tip of his nose pointing towards the stagnant wings of the ceiling fan.

"They want us to leave. Chacha has found a smuggler who flies people out."

Hope bloomed in Neelo's heart, but before she allowed it to blossom, she asked, "can we all really leave?" What was left of their family, she wanted to hold close.

"Not all of us, Neelo. Just the two of us."

Her hope dissipated with a painful sting.

"We can't leave them. We can't be the ones who get to escape."

They did escape in the end, after Ammi fell to her knees and leaned at Neelo's feet, begging her to save herself, and when Chacha tightly gripped Zafar's shoulders and asked him to save the family- to not let them all be extinguished by this war.

Zafar began his life in the foggy city with earnest and a determination to move forward. Where they came from, even during the war, the air swelled with the resounding and melodic call to prayer five times a day, inviting them to the mosque. Here, the call was silent, but he answered anyway. The mosque was where he found community.

Neelo, however, was caught in limbo. She paced their apartment day and night, her bare feet treading the same path. Despite Zafar's gentle coaxing and his stories of the mosque, the teeming farmer's market and the volunteers at the Refugee Welcome Association, Neelo remained inside. Her mind was buried in the past.

Neelo woke up one morning to find a child perched on the kitchen counter. It was a girl with solemn dark eyes shaped like almonds. Her legs hung from the edge and her hands folded in her lap. She could have been a statue.

Neelo was more curious than startled. Her questions met with silence and with each question the silence deepened. The last vestiges of sleep hung in her heavy eyelids and in the sourness of her mouth. Impatience stirred in her chest- impatience with this strange child in the kitchen of this strange house in a country and a city so strange and new.

She moved closer and reached out to touch the girl's shoulder. Her fingers passed frigid air. The cold seeped into her fingertips, swirled in her blood and gripped her heart. Neelo ran and slammed the bedroom door shut, erecting a barrier between her and the child who was not really there.

There was a spirit in her house. She sat by the door for a while, still and unmoving. Her nightgown was splayed by her side and her arms clutched her knees. When she gathered trepid courage and opened the bedroom door, through the sliver she saw that the girl had moved from the kitchen counter to the window. Arms folded at her chest, she gazed out the window, standing still in a shaft of sunlight streaming in. She didn't have a shadow.

Neelo's scar throbbed and ached.

Was the ghost of this child with almond eyes taunting her vacant arms that once held Annie?

When Zafar returned that night, the sun had already set and the child fell into the shadows and disappeared. Neelo did not know if she had imagined it all. Was it the past playing tricks with her mind?

She returned the next morning, and this time, Neelo was a little less startled. It continued this way for weeks. The girl with olive skin and almond-shaped dark eyes became Neelo's silent companion and each night she disappeared with the setting sun right before Zafar returned, and Neelo never told him.

Zafar woke up first. The apartment had already filled with smoke, but there was no sign of fire yet. When he shook Neelo awake, she had at the bottom, and the oval of a waning blue sky loomed above, taunting her with freedom. She frantically searched for the iron rungs of a ladder, but her fingers only found cold, damp stone.

She woke up stunned and afraid, clutching at Zafar's night shirt. He held her all the way down the stairs and out into the dark night, where they gulped their first lungful of clean air. The blanket that only moments ago covered their sleeping bodies was now draped over them.

The dark sky camouflaged the billowing smoke. It was the house on the left that had caught fire, the wind encouraging the flames to engulf and destroy. The three houses would crumble soon. In the morning when the rain came, only charred husks would be left standing. Dark ash would flow to the streets in black rivulets.

In the chaos, the heat of the blaze hissed at Neelo's skin. Crowds gathered buckets of sand and water to douse the flames. Hollers and screams rang in the night. She scanned the dark windows of the other houses spewing smoke and flames for signs of life, she thought of the girl who was frigid air. Could a fire burn someone who was not there?

Zafar held Neelo as the flames blazed stronger. Through the turmoil, carried on the strong wind was the unmistakable sound of a baby crying. It came from the top window of the house on the left.

It happened within a split fraction of time. Zafar draped the blanket over his head and dove into the flaming house. As all time slowed and the chaos deepened, Neelo saw him emerge again, the blanket now wrapped around a bundle in his charred hands. A child lost and a child saved. As Neelo ran to him, she saw what he carried in his arms was a wailing baby. Her skin was olive, and her eyes shaped like almonds.

Megan Munn

A proud supporter of the Oxford Comma, Megan has been reading writing, and editing since she was a child. Her favourite stories include elements of fantasy, science fiction, mystery, and the supernatural. Megan graduated with a Bachelor of Arts and a Bachelor of Education, majoring in English Literature, with a desire to teach Shakespeare. While struggling to complete a full novel, Megan as written numerous short stories and poems. In her spare time, she likes to cosplay, craft, and game. She considers herself to be a well-rounded geek with too many hobbies.

Sirens screeched in the dusk in this foggy city I call home. Today the fog was supplemented with acrid smoke rising from the shattered windows and rooftop of the house on the corner of Charlotte and St. James Street. Aside from the smoke and fire, it almost looked like a larger version of the house beside it. I sometimes wondered if the person who designed these buildings had made the larger as an apartment, building the smaller as their own house. Now the small one stood empty, a Century 21 sign nailed to the siding.

I stood barefoot across the street, a disheveled mess with burnt pajama pants and an old t-shirt, numbly watching as the flames spread within the windows, outside the windows, and onto the grey clapboard siding. I hoped the sirens would turn into fire engines soon. I didn't want another Great Fire spreading through the city like it did back in 1877. It was probably the most significant event in all of our foggy city's history. A derisive laugh escaped my throat. It seemed like I was tempting fate remembering such a thing right now.

A gust of wind fanned the flames. My hair blew around my face, tickling the back of my neck. I raked my nails up and down to ease the itch. They were back. The itch spread. Down my back, up my legs, across my shoulders, through my arms, weaving through the hairs on my scalp. It didn't matter how much I scratched. The itch was like the guilt eating away at me from deep in my gut.

It's not my fault.

The thought caught in my throat, choking me like the smoke in my apartment.

It wasn't my fault.I may have started the fire, but it wasn't my fault.

It was a little closer to the truth. I should have been more careful. I shouldn't have overreacted.

I was just trying to protect myself.

But did I really need to protect myself like that? Wasn't that a wee bit irresponsible?

Of course not! It's not like I wanted to set the building on fire.

Then again, they did catch me off guard.

Those bastards!

I was terrified. Can you blame me?

Those bastards! It's all their fault!

If only they hadn't shown up. If only they would just leave me alone. Why can't I live my life in peace? They had to be there, hiding in the shadows, perched in anticipation of my arrival, bating me in my moment of weakness when I failed to double check my surroundings.

Earlier that evening, I just wanted peace and

quiet. I dimmed the lighting in the living room. The brightness compounded my headache, a remnant from a stressful day at work. My ears ached from the headphones and the jabs from irate customers who didn't seem to remember that they were dealing with another human being on the other end of the line. In a blue-collar city, it was only natural to be working a call-centre job.

I lit the candles, one on either side of me and one on the table in front of me. I rolled out the yoga mat straight and neat on the hardwood floor. Barefoot, I stood and took a deep breath, determined to try Ujjayi breathing without the video aid. I knew I needed to be able to do this on my own, at any time. I couldn't keep having anxiety attacks at work. And so I took my stance - feet together, standing straight, palms touching as if in prayer - and prepared for the zen that I so desired.

Why did they have to be there?

First one, then the other. They dropped down from above, hovering in front of me, reaching for me, their long legs and sticky webs ready to attack, to pierce through my peaceful thoughts. My breath caught in my throat. I was suffocating.

I always knew they were conspiring against me. But it had been so long. I let myself relax. I let down my guard.

They were in my hair now. I fell backward,

knocking a candle over. I could feel them running up my legs and back. They tried to climb into my ears. I waved my hands around me, up and down my body, trying to wipe them all off. Where were they?! I couldn't see them. I knew they were there, I could feel them, but I couldn't see them. Nails dug into skin as I tried to swipe them away, to make the itching stop

The candle was burning, flame leaking out onto the floor, catching the yoga mat, catching my pants. I had to do something. There were spiders all over me. I needed to get them off.

Cold water splashed from the kitchen tap into the sink. I cupped my hands under the stream and threw the cleansing liquid all over me: first my flaming pants, then my face, my neck, and my arms, scrubbing myself with my palms. I knew my hair was causing the itch, causing me to believe they were there when they were not. I gripped a fistful, pain piercing my scalp. A hot burn erupted on my calf. I hadn't felt the fire, I just reacted. I needed something to cool it. Splashing water wasn't enough.

I reached for a dish towel as the shrill sound of the fire alarm went off. It was too late to stop it on my own. Dousing the cloth in cold water, I wrapped it around the burn and barely managed to tie it off. My next thoughts were of escaping the building.

The smoke was rising. I felt my throat closing up,

burning. Suppressing a cough, I raced to the door, not thinking until too late to check the knob for warmth. Thank goodness the fire was behind me. The knob was cool. It turned easily. I swung the door open, and it crashed into the wall. Other tenants were opening their doors, curious as to the sound of the fire alarm. I ignored them. My smoke-filled lungs held no capacity to talk, to yell at them to run. I hoped my actions would suffice. Into the hallway, water dripping down my burnt leg and under my bare foot, I slid on the hardwood. I reached for the wall beside me, steadying myself.

In that instant, I looked back. The blaze was brilliant. It was so bright that tears budded in my stinging eyes. The spiders were in those flames.

Die.

Die diediediediediediedie.

Those bastards got what they deserved. The fire would incinerate them on their way to hell. If only it didn't mean my life was also going up in flames.

I escaped across the hallway and down the stairs. The other tenants were clamouring to get out as well. Parents were gathering children, the elderly tenants stumbled, and younger tenants reached out to help. People were on their cell phones dialing 911.

We made it out. We crossed the street and waited for the sirens to arrive. The tears caused by the brightness of the flames had leaked down my cheeks. They were no longer tears of visual pain alone. The weight in my stomach, like a tide of acid, threatened to roar up my throat. The back of my neck itched. The thought of those spiders following me, surviving with me, gripped the edges of my mind. I scratched and fought it off.

There's no way they could have survived. I killed them all. They burst into flames. They were dead, dead!

I was finally safe; I could finally have peace.

I watched, numb to the noise, as the fire truck pulled up in front of the house. The firemen shooed us all away so they could do their job. One of them asked if I was okay. I smiled at him.

"I'm fine. They're all dead, so I'm fine."

Grayson O'Hearn

Grayson has always had his head in the clouds, or shall we say, in a whole other world. While not originally from Saint John, Grayson grew up in a small fishing village in eastern Nova Scotia, nestled in the perfect mixture of ocean and forest to spark an active imagination. With a love of fantasy literature and a longing for an escape to the magical and unnatural, he set his sights on writing, focusing the ideas and dreams in his head into creating worlds and magic on paper. After all what is a book but a gateway into a different life?

A Window Behind the Fog

A small lady wandered the streets of the foggy city. She often went unnoticed by the many inhabitants of the city. Her face told a story of all the years she has seen with every wrinkle, spot, and scar. A single strand of grey hair hung down onto her black attire from the bun that kept it off her shoulders. Stopping at an old concrete box of a house, with symmetrical pillars at its entrance and a tiny outcrop at its peak with a small stained-glass window, she revealed an old key from her pocket. Crows had begun to gather in the trees and on the power lines in front of the house, watching as she went inside.

From the street, the house was ordinary; it didn't quite match the architecture of the houses around it, but it was typical in every other way. Inside, however, was a very different story. Once past the foyer where the woman hung up her shawl and kicked off her shoes, there was a large staircase with a small black door on either side. The air in the house was stale. Cobwebs and dust accented the corners of the room and cast a soft grey tone on the old books on the shelves. At the top of the stairs above the door sat a small perch where a large raven stared down at anyone who entered.

"Hello my dear," the woman called to it as it gave her a loud and sharp greeting. The raven hopped along the perch gleefully before swooping down to land on her sunken shoulders. Together they shambled through the small black door and into another room dimly lit by candles and colourful liquids stewing in various cast iron pots. The woman slumped into an ornate chair beside one of the pots and stared at it as she spoke to the raven at her side.

"The spirits are out today; they hung in the fog trying for someone's attention, wailing like the wind. Once again, no one could hear them. The people of this city are kind but they don't have the sight to see what surrounds them. They can't see what lies in the fog whenever it comes," the woman said emphatically. "If only I could go over to the island unseen, I could ease their pain again for a while, before they become too restless."

She sat for a moment and pondered before she snapped her fingers and jumped from her seat, startling the raven.

"I've got it Eldritch, we'll use a simple soothing spell like we did back in 1877 when the spirits became restless after the fire. It should send most of them back to the island where they came from. That'll give me time to get these old bones over there to properly soothe them."

She rushed over to a dusty bookshelf that looked as if it could collapse at any moment and pulled out an old black book labeled *Beatrice's Grimoire*. She shuffled through it remarking to Eldritch that her notes looked like bird scratchings and jokingly asked if it had actually been him that had written them. He gave a loud squawk and ruffled his feathers at her.

Beatrice stopped on an old tea-stained page with the headline *Soothing Shadows,* thinking it would be just the thing to do the trick. She had no doubt that these spirits, more complex than mere shadows, would not be put to rest, but the spell would calm them down enough to be manageable. She began gathering the ingredients from her stores: a sprig of lavender plucked from a plant that grew against all odds, six drops of slug slime, the feather of a dove pure and white, and lastly a stone washed and polished in the waters of the Dead Sea. All the ingredients were thrown into her most ornate pot, gilded with gold and the rim of polished fluorite. As the ingredients boiled, Beatrice recited a few words over them as Eldritch squawked along musically at her shoulder.

Lavender to soothe your hearts and put you to a melancholic rest, the Slime of Slug to slow the anguish in your minds, the Feather of a Dove to lighten your burdens and guide you to your grave, A stone washed in the waters of the salted sea to make you pure once more. Cauldron boil, cauldron simmer, show me your secret face- Cauldron bubble, cauldron glimmer, make these spirits leave no trace.

When the liquid turned from a putrid green colour to a glorious and beautiful white gold, the brewing process was a success. Now all she had to do was leave the brew in the moonlight overnight to gather its energy.

At sunrise, as Eldritch stared at it unblinking with his beady black eyes, she scooped it out into three large vials and put them in an old sack.

"Now Eldritch, all we have to do is put these on the edges of the city and wait for the fog to roll back in. Maybe you could convince some of those nosy old crows outside to help out for a change instead of staring at me all day," she yelled in a sharp tone.

Beatrice set the old bag by the door and ascended the stairs to the small outcrop that led to the rest of the house. She wandered down the hall until she stopped at an old stairwell that led to the attic, huffing with every step and remarking at the top that she was getting too old for this. Beatrice made her way through the narrow attic until she was in front of the old stained-glass window. Colourful fractals of light streamed in and rested on her withered face. In the light she felt young again and if anyone had been watching, they would have seen a young woman basking in colourful rays of warm sunlight and not the old woman that she really was.

Strange things happen in places you would least expect them. The unseen and the unknown are always swirling just beyond our reach. They are in alleyways that we turn our heads from, the birds that gather to wait for the storm, or even a window that rejuvenates the soul and transforms sunlight into a fountain of youth for all who bask in its golden brilliance. Beatrice held on dearly to the powers that her window gave her. Made by a powerful witch from the 1600's, it held a magic that she could never hope to replicate and she coveted it with her life. If it were ever to shatter, she would have to grow old and pass on like the mortals in the city around her.

Beatrice gathered herself from the light of the window and like a butterfly, finally emerging from its cocoon, she took a few staggered steps before bouncing with newfound energy down the stairs. Missing a step in the excitement, she landed face first on the dusty wooden floor. Eldritch ruffled his feathers once more and hopped over to pick at her hair.

"Well, Eldritch, let's go.I'll have just enough time to make it to the corners of the city before the sun sets," she crooned, dragging herself off the floor and down the stairs. "If we get separated, be back before midnight." The raven pecked at her, annoyed at her remark, as if she was implying this was their first time adventuring away from the magic of the window. They made their way out of the house and into the cold maritime air, clouds of hot vapour forming in front of them as they walked.

As Beatrice locked her door, she could hear the squawking all around her. More crows had gathered in the square and on the eaves of her own house.

She was cautious of them at first, but an aggressive caw from Eldritch made most of them fly away in fear.

Being a woman with little means of transportation, Beatrice often walked or took public transit. She made her way through the bustling streets and up towards the woodlands of Rockwood Park, Eldritch keeping watch from high above her so the pair didn't draw too much attention. The spring air had only just begun to settle into the park. Many of the lakes and ponds were still covered in a thin sheet of ice. The frosted pools of water nestled in the trees were the perfect point to place the first of the vials. Setting her sights on a tree rooted on a small piece of land just off the shore, she called Eldritch down to carry it over and nestle it among the foliage.

Another was to be placed in the woodlands of Taylors Island on the west side. Beatrice had to take the bus to get there and the thought alone made her queasy. As she boarded the bus she greeted the driver with an anxious smile and the familiar rattle of change as she dropped her coins into the box. Beatrice always sat in the back of the bus when she could so no one would notice if she gained a few years on the journey. When she reached the last stop before the park, she braced herself for the long walk ahead of her.

By the time she reached the still-cool shores of Saint's Rest Beach, framed by the rocky edges of

Taylors Island, she stood for a long while taking in the sight and sound of the waves and the salt spray on her skin. Several paces up an embankment and into the trees, Beatrice found the perfect place for the vial. She nestled it in a tree beside some very curious squirrels. On the way back to the bus stop and on her way home, Eldritch was tasked with flying the third and final vial out to Anthonys Cove. It was too far for Beatrice to go to herself in one day and well outside the city.

The day was waning and the sun setting before they returned back to their cozy home. Eldritch was tired and Beatrice's body had began to wilt as the years returned to her; the rose of a woman she had been in the day became the bleeding heart that she was at night. The crows had gone by nightfall, but their feathers were scattered on the street around her home.

The stiffness of the air in her house was a welcoming feeling: it gave her a sense of security and peace, one place she could always relax at her leisure when she wasn't protecting the city she called home. Slumping into her favourite chair, she was asleep in mere minutes, the soft breathing of Eldritch above her wrapped up in his own dreams. Beatrice's dreams were filled with all her worries and fears that she had pushed from her waking mind. When she was just a young girl, before migrating to Canada, she and her family had lived in Salem. She was only 12 when the witch trials had taken place. In her dreams she remembered vividly what fear of the unknown does to people. So many of her family friends had been accused, but none of the women sentenced to death had actually been real witches. It was from that moment she decided to protect people from ever having to come to terms with the things they didn't understand. She only wanted to keep the peace and ease their minds.

When Beatrice had settled in the small coastal city of Saint John, she and her mother enjoyed an unnaturally long life due to the magic of Helena Claire. She was the very same woman who had made the stained-glass window. Her mother and Helena had decided that the world was becoming tedious and unfamiliar so they made the decision to pass on naturally, but they couldn't ask Beatrice to do the same. In their final days they used their combined magic to form a brilliant stained-glass window out of sand they had gathered on one of the beaches near the city. They forged the window with blue flames, charged it under a full red harvest moon, and cooled it in the salty waters that kissed the shores. The window was installed in their family home at the very top level and both Helena and Beatrice's mother passed their magic onto the window, making it a vessel of power and youth, the strengths of the women that had left their mark on it.

"Beatrice, you must sit under this window once a day to feel fully rejuvenated. The sunlight and moonlight that streams through it will charge the air in the house with our magic. It won't be enough to let you leave the house so you must absorb its light directly," were the final words Beatrice's mother spoke to her as she and Helena left the house and were never seen again.

For years she was angry at her mother and Helena for leaving her alone. They gave her the parting gift of the window to keep her alive and young as long as she was in the house, but that couldn't cure her loneliness. It was then that she decided she would conjure a familiar, and in 1952 Eldritch was summoned by giving shape and form to a piece of her own soul, and the two were bonded ever since.

When morning came the crows had flocked to the streets outside. A chorus of loud and grating caws echoing between several crows. Beatrice was rattled by the noise of Eldritch screeching back at them as he woke. Wiping her eyes, she flicked the bird from her chair with a small piece of parchment that had been lying on her desk.

"You silly bird, you scared me half to death! What have I told you about making noise in my ears this early in the morning?" Beatrice scolded.

She shuffled to her feet and out to the street in her slippers, stopping at the cold wall of fog that greeted her and hung heavily over the city. The crows surrounding her home were twisting and turning their heads in every direction, getting startled by things that a normal person may not see.

When they noticed her step out of her house they turned their attention only to her, watching intently for her next move. Eldritch swooped out from the darkness of the house and onto a post beside his most valued companion.

"Do you see them?" She gestured to the fog, the raven giving a soft coo in response.

"They're startling the birds, the first sign that they have begun to grab at the living world. There are so many of them, so I hope this works. If it doesn't, I say we blame those lazy crows." Beatrice threw her hands up at the crows in the trees and returned to her study. She dragged out the old black book once more and brought it to the attic, settling herself in front of the window, basking in its light to harness its power on top of her own. Returning to the page labeled *Soothing Shadows,* she scrolled a single finger down the old parchment and over the inked black letters until she came to the bottom of the page. The final enchantment would tie the whole spell together and connect the vials she had placed throughout the city with her location.

Her breathing became heavy and sweat began to collect on her brow. Even though she had done similar spells countless times before, she still got nervous whenever the time came to do another. Beatrice never believed in herself and was never sure enough in her abilities to have the confidence of the women that came before her. Helena used to tell her growing up that she thought one day she might surpass even her if she gave herself enough of a chance, but Beatrice thought that was absurd. She thought to herself, *how could a woman that can barely brew a simple potion surpass Helena, a woman that could give youth and hold death at bay?*

She remembered how calm Helena was when they first escaped to Canada and spent the winter trying to survive in Canadian wilds, conjuring fire like it was nothing and growing food through the snow. Helena's strength was manipulating nature, but to Beatrice she had no weakness, she excelled at everything and failed at nothing - something she felt that she would never measure up to. While Helena made surviving seem easy that winter, Beatrice almost got herself killed by a particularly angry mother black bear with a handful of young. She froze in fear and had to be rescued by the older women because she was too afraid to use a calming spell on them.

Beatrice shook the thought and the doubt from her mind and began to recite the words as assertive as she could towards the glimmering window. The thought of not being able to calm the bear back then gave her the strength and determination to calm the restless spirits of the city now.

Spirits unseen and spirits in agony, let us prevent anymore tragedy. Heed my warning and hear my call. Go back to your rest, lay stiff like a doll. With the breaking of vials and the call of the grave, Leave this place like a thunderous wave.

The wind had picked up around the house. The wailing of several spirits shook the trees of their black-feathered guests and enveloped the house like thousands of crashing waves in a tropical storm. Beatrice stood her ground, envisioning her will to be stronger than the spirits that threatened her. Eldritch puffed himself up on the windowsill creating an amusing silhouette in the colourful glass, although Beatrice assumed, he thought he was the picture of intimidation. The house shook more and more until things began to fall from shelves and the sound of glass shattering could be heard from downstairs. Still, her feet firmly set, she was determined to keep her focus. When the spirits had finally passed by her house and the wind had started to die down, she allowed herself to relax. Even Eldritch seemed tired from puffing himself up in the window. As the two of them turned to leave the attic, something registered in Beatrice's mind that made her heart sink and filled her with fear she'd never truly felt since the days of the witch trials.

The shattering of glass so near had seemed so far away as she had detached herself from reality. Afraid to look, she stood frozen, facing down the stairwell into the floor below. It was the fear one gets in the dark when they can feel the silent stare of something looking back at them: chills are sent up your spine and you feel exposed to the unforgiving darkness.

She had to look; she had to work up the courage to turn around. She called for her raven under her breath and he nuzzled his head into the crook in her neck to comfort her.

Slowly, she turned on her heels to peer out into the open landscape of the city before her. Under any other circumstance, she might find the view a beauty to behold, but the view meant nothing to her but the end of her years. The stained-glass window that once shone and sparkled in the glorious sunlight was now little more than dusty edges and jagged shapes strew out across the wooden beams of the attic floor. In the centre of the pieces laid a large crow. Her sorrow for herself was quickly replaced by the sorrow for the crow that had met its end on her floor. She may have found them annoying, but she loved them as she did any living thing. Scooping it up, she brought it to her study.

“Poor thing didn't mean to come crashing through my window, but I guess we have to help it now, don't we, Eldritch? We only have a short time left before its soul leaves its body and once that happens, there’s no coming back,” she spoke cautiously.

Beatrice laid the crow’s limp form on her desk and ran her fingers across the dust covered vials that lined the shelves above her books. She stopped on one filled with a dark purple liquid that looked like a bottled galaxy and put three drops on the crow’s crown.

One drop for life. One drop for rejuvenation. And a final for luck.

Her words were almost echoing in the room as the crow's wings began to flap and its body and bones mended before their eyes. The crow gave a loud squawk and shook itself off as it scanned the room, confused. Eldritch hopped on the desk beside it and spoke to the crow in a series of loud caws before returning to Beatrice's shoulder. Much to her surprise, the crow took note and hopped onto her other shoulder as well, and the three of them made their way out onto the street.

Many of the crows had returned to the trees and eaves now that the spirits had gone and they seemed to rejoice at the return of one of their own, circling the woman and landing at her feet. They were grateful, they were happy, and most importantly they were in her debt.

"It brings a tear to my eyes to see such a change in all you lazy old..." She stopped herself and adjusted her tone, "in all you beautiful crows. It seems all these years we simply misunderstood and distrusted each other when we could have been working together. Regardless, the past is the past. Watch over this city for me when I'm gone: that will be your debt to me. Whenever someone sees a crow, perhaps they will feel safe. They may not know you're there to watch over them, but if you do a good enough job by them, they will understand. Take care of the city." Beatrice watched the crows as they flew off in flocks over the bright morning clouds and off into the city. The house she knew and loved for so long, she now looked at with fond memories.

"Well, Eldritch, we have a little work to do yet. Will you stay with me until the end?" she asked him somberly. He stared at her intently so she would know he was with her as the two returned inside for the last time. She made her way slowly through the house, and into her study, remarking on all the things that had made her life so blissful in her 339 years. The old black and white photos of her, her mother and Helena going on adventures in the Maritimes, the sketches they had drawn by an artist in Massachusetts when she was just a girl with her original coven, and finally a large painting she had attempted herself of Eldritch when he was small. Her memories unraveled in the small room she had spent so much time in, but she had to let it all go. Flipping through the pages of her grimoire she ended on the final spell and recited it with great regret.

When I am gone, I leave no trace- Wipe all memory of me from this place. Within these walls I never wept, Within these walls I will never again step. When I'm gone, don't leave a trace- Wipe all memory of me from this place.

By the time she finished the incantation her face

was wet with tears. She was the last of her coven, and there was no one around to know where she went or how much she had done for them. She had never needed recognition; all she wanted was someone to love her and miss her when she was gone. Her thoughts were quickly broken by Eldritch nuzzling himself into her neck and nibbling playfully on her earlobe.

"I always could count on you, Eldritch. You truly were the best familiar a woman could ever ask for, and the most loving and understanding friend I could have ever hoped for. It's time to go. Are you ready?" she asked him while scratching under his beak.

Saint John seemed to be bustling more than usual as the pair left their house for the final time. They walked along the uptown streets accepting the strange looks of anyone who passed them. A little boy walking with his mother stopped to tell her how cool he thought it was that she had a pet crow. She quickly corrected him and assured him that Eldritch was not her pet but her friend and that he was a raven, not a crow, and the interaction made her happy. She then thought it wasn't so bad to be noticed and stared at. She had always been taught not to be seen or draw any attention to herself but perhaps the warnings of her mother were misguided in the 21st century. Maybe in another life witches would have been accepted instead of feared.

When Beatrice finally arrived at the shoreline and

looked out onto the rocky bridge that stood in the way of her and the island she was headed to, she was glad that the effects of the window hadn't completely left her. She tossed the raven from her shoulder to better her balance and he soared high into the sky to keep watch over her as she went. With every step she became more unsteady and she noticed as she fumbled and shook across the rocks that veins and wrinkles had began to resurface on her skin. The crashing waves on either side of her were a constant reminder of the gravity of the situation.

Once over the final outcropping of rocks, Beatrice's frail frame collapsed on the solid ground of Partridge Island, the lighthouse towering above her wavering in her dizzy state. She had passed out for several minutes before the pecking of a familiar beak at her hair roused her.

"I know, I know; I'm not allowed to give up yet. I do far too much for far too little reward, you know that?" she scoffed.

It was all she could do to crawl up to the centre of the island and dig a balled-up piece of parchment from the pocket of her pants, a page she had ripped from her book of spells before she left. Her hands now curled unwillingly around the piece of parchment as her rapidly aging body struggled to unfold it. She took one final deep breath and knew that what she was about to do would make sure that the city she had dedicated her life to protecting, would never again be plagued by wondering spirits.

Sealing spirits with a soul lock restless spirits understand what I say- You shall no longer be allowed to stay. In your grave is where you rest. But in this will be your final test. With my soul willingly given, I banish you to the lands beyond – Its time to leave and say goodbye, its time for you to be gone.

A great rift opened in the sky above the island and a stark and brilliant white light poured down on Beatrice and Eldritch. As the spirits began to disappear around them one by one a shockwave of energy was sent out from the pair that traveled for miles out into the bay and the city behind them. The island was sealed and as Beatrice and Eldritch faded into oblivion, a smile could be seen on her face. If anyone had been there to look at her they would have seen a woman basking in the brilliance of the warm sunlight and maybe if they looked close enough they would see a woman who, in her own way, surpassed the goals that her predecessor Helena had set for her. She was no longer just Beatrice, she was the woman that gave her entire life to protecting others for no recognition, in a world that had only ever showed her cruelty and misunderstanding. She was happy and at peace as she faded from the world, her energy dissipating and merging with the energy around her.

As the months passed, eventually people

wondered about the vacant house in the middle of the street. The neighbours could never remember anyone living there but knew that someone must have. It was put up for sale and renovations were eventually done. What used to be the round stained-glass window that was the focal point of the building, became three small square windows. The house was modernized and changed to match the architecture of the surrounding neighbours and eventually became only a shadow of its former antiquity, but if you look closely enough at the roof you might just notice it. Some say the crows still gather there from time to time, keeping their promise to Beatrice and her feathered familiar to always watch over anyone in need.

Andalice Storey

Andalice writes General Fiction, YA, Historical Fiction, and rewriting classic Greek short stories with a modern twist between raising her kids and making homemade meals for her partner and family. Three things about her: she will save the skunk no one else would dare to, she never gives up on what is important to her, and she like to hug trees. She lives in Saint John and Salisbury, in New Brunswick. This is her first published short story.

The Wharf Master's Daughter

And the Stone Carver's Son

She rubbed the sleep out of her eyes and stared at the ceiling. It was the same light fixture from when she was little, the one her father had installed when she was six. Her parents' bedroom still smelled of old wallpaper glue and dust. The flowers used to be violet but had faded to pale grey-blue over the decades. For a moment, she felt like nothing had changed and that if she turned her head, her mother would be there breathing, next to her, or there leaning against the doorframe with a hot cup of coffee in her hand, smiling. The day before when she arrived at her mother's home, she stood beside her mother's favourite green and gold embroidered ottoman and stared at the empty chair.

Anastasia O'Brien wiped her eyes as she came to terms with the cold absence of her mother. The night before, she was overridden with grief and had climbed into her mother, Bethany O'Brien's, bed. She found comfort between the sheets that hadn't been changed since her death. The smell of soap and cigarette smoke wafted about each time Anastasia moved. That did it. She wanted to wrap herself up in that smell forever.

The phone rang. The sound was coming from the bathroom. She tried to untangle herself from the multiple layers of blankets. "Too. Many. Layers," she murmured.

Balancing on one foot, she grabbed at the bedsheet that wouldn't let go, as though a last line to the past, and toppled over. She landed on the dusty floral rug with a thud that her mother would've laughed at.

The phone stopped ringing.

What a way to start the day; she marched down the corridor, into the bathroom and checked her messages. It was work. She decided that her job could wait. She had a full two weeks' leave of absence, and she needed every minute of it.

She got dressed and ready for the day. The photograph of her and her mother on the bureau seemed to portray a time lost in history, yet she could feel how joyous her mother was in that moment. Bethany had been a stately woman with short, strawberry-blonde hair and clear blue eyes. And to any adoring daughter, she seemed something like an Irish queen. She was proud to have the same hair and fair complexion as her mother, but she was very short, with tiny ankles and big, awkward hands.

Anastasia planned to make her way to the funeral parlour, deliver Bethany her mother's eulogy, avoid Kirk Trueman, her father Charles O'Brien - that's if he showed up at all - and anyone that reminded her of her past. Her insecurities and past demons seemed so great, yet so ordinary. She counted the days until she was back home.

She'd make her excuses as early as possible without seeming rude, go back to her mother's house – now hers – and clear out the fridge. Then she'd spend the evening drinking as much gin as her body could tolerate. The next morning, she'd find a realtor and a manager for the tenants, list and sell the damn house along with the tiny gargoyles atop the edge of the roof that her father had carved out of stone. It wouldn't take long to bid all three tenants goodbye and good luck, make her final exit, and never look back.

Selling was logical; she couldn't just quit and leave work. Many fond memories were etched in her heart but she had no reason to stay. Once the house sold, she'd return to her own life: taking care of seniors, and painting at night. She was used to her small house and her life on the edge of the city in Perth, Ontario.

Queen Square North, Saint John, New Brunswick, was the place where her father left her and her mother, and shortly after ended up in jail for a while because of his abusive behaviour toward the family. The first incorporated city of Canada was the place where she fell in love with her best friend, Kirk, at Lloyd's Slip. It was where they had mapped out a course for their lives and future. But he changed his mind and married Cassandra.

It was Bethany who destroyed Anastasia and Kirk's future when she told her daughter that Kirk was Anastasia's half-brother. Sure, Kirk had some similar physical characteristics as Charles O'Brien, but there are many people in the world with similar features. It didn't mean they were related. She spoke to Kirk about it. All he'd said was "sorry" and walked away. For months Anastasia prodded her mother while Kirk and his new fiancée were planning their wedding. She accused her mother of being the one who told Kirk, which she denied, and finally she had to let it go when Kirk married Cassandra.

She shook hands with Kirk, briefly wondering where his wife was. Maybe he was sparing her the pain of seeing him with Cassandra at her own mother's funeral.

"Anastasia," Kirk swallowed.

Her neck felt a tingle. It had been years since she heard him say her name.

"Can we talk?" asked Kirk.

Not in this lifetime was what her mouth opened to say, but she bit her tongue instead.

As though her tongue was still pinched, she blurted out, "maybe later."

Her Auntie Georgie was playing hostess, which was a relief. She asked everyone to gather in the main room.

Anastasia hurried off before Kirk could say another word. The funeral director caught up to her to inform her they'd soon be finishing up and invited her to rejoin the group. Was she avoiding Kirk, or her mother's service?

She quietly settled in the reserved seat at the front. A few cousins she had occasionally spent time with during family gatherings came over and sat with her. The service was the longest thirty minutes of her life. She couldn't wait to get out of there.

After people hugged her, whispered their condolences, and rushed off to eat and casually chat at the buffet table, Tawny Haggerty, her mother's old friend, brought over a small canister full of cookies and told her to open it. On top of the cookies was a piece of parchment and folded inside a letter addressed to Bethany O'Brien.

Anastasia studied the envelope.

"What's this, Tawny?"

"You know your mother. So secretive..." She pecked Anastasia on the cheek. "She told me to give this to you if she, er... when she..." Tawny looked at the photograph next to the urn and swallowed. Anastasia steadied her nerves and did not look in that direction. Tawny's eyes were red-rimmed, turning them a startling shade of green.

"Passed on," said Anastasia with a sigh.

"You look tired, dear. You getting enough sleep?"

Familiar felt good. "Enough," she lied.

Tawny stood up, cocked an eyebrow. "You call me..."

"...if I need anything. Yeah, I know, Tawny."

Her heart pounded. A letter her mother only dared to give her after her death. There was only one thing she ever felt her mother hid from her, and it was about Kirk.

"Tawny?"

"No Annie, I didn't read it. You know I'd tell you to prepare yourself for something wonderful or dreadful if I knew, but I don't."

"That's okay, Tawny. Thanks for being a true friend."

"You bet. Call me anytime."

Anastasia smiled.

The ceremony and eulogy went well enough. She shook people's hands on the way, and thanked them. That was when she saw Kirk smiling at her by the funeral parlour's entrance.

"How do you like Perth?" Kirk asked.

Flushed and jittery, Anastasia replied, “It’s nice.”

“Less cold in the winter, I imagine?”

“Yeah.”

“Listen, you and me….”

“Kirk, I don’t know…” She licked her lips.

Anastasia sensed Kirk looking at her as a stroke of visceral sadness caught her breath. He was looking at her with anchoring eyes, digging deep into her as his eyes once did. It was tearing her insides out.

“How’s Cassandra?”

Kirk’s eyelids flinched and looked down. That was the bomb. He coughed.

“I want to – ” he began.

The funeral director turned the corner.

“Oh, I’m sorry. I didn’t know anyone was still here.”

“We were just leaving,” said Anastasia staring at Kirk who smiled awkwardly.

Two days after her mother’s funeral, a ‘For Sale’ sign posted on the side of the house left Anastasia discouraged and feeling guilty because her mother’s lawyer told her that Bethany’s last wishes were that her daughter would live in her house and to take over the rental. She had gone through years of bills and rent receipts. The rent had stayed the same for over a decade, while the bills had gone up, not to mention her mother had re-mortgaged the house when her father left them. It was how she could afford sailing school and many other things. At the time, Anastasia had thought that they were doing well. Plus, her mother sewed for a few clients off and on throughout the years and washed all the tenants' laundry for only twenty dollars per family.

She eyed the letter and read the excerpt:

...We both know the child is mine and I worry for you that Charles will not accept our daughter as his own. He has done you wrong getting Mrs. Trueman pregnant, but now I feel we were no better. We will wait and hope that she takes your physical characteristics - if not, darling then I do not know what to do. We both know I cannot leave my own wife and nine children. I wish you well and am truly sorry for your predicament.

H. Fogart

"Henry Fogart," she whispered. "The old wharf master." Mr. Fogart had often watched Anastasia and Kirk loitering at the harbour countless times and said nothing. Now she knew why.

Somehow, Kirk had found out his father was Charles O'Brien during the summer she was away learning to sail in B.C. Kirk hadn't been there beside her mother to receive her when she returned. He was supposed to be there; he'd promised her.

"Dear," Bethany had said that day, "Kirk fell in love with Cassandra while you were away. The scoundrel," she puffed on her cigarette. "Didn't I tell you there wasn't an honest bone in that boy's body?"

Anastasia returned the letter to its envelope and closed her eyes. Her mother had thrown the news into her face like a headline. A real gossip pieces. She and Kirk had made promises to one another and, just like that, it was over.

Somewhere between Kirk's promise to her and his freedom that summer, he supposedly fell in love with Cassandra and married her a few weeks after Anastasia came back in September. Cassandra was a pretty, rich girl. Anastasia's hopes and dreams sunk to the bottom of the harbour like gold lost in the murkiest water.

Crossed legged and eating toast on the broad bay windowsill, she tried to image how things might go between her and Kirk but it was better that she suppressed delusions. This was going to be harder than she thought, since she obviously still had strong feelings for him.

She leaned against her calico cushions. It'd soon be Christmas again and there was no way she'd spend it here, no matter how much fun Uptown Sparkles was. Less than a week to go. The tree lighting, singing carols, sipping hot chocolate, and visiting all the participating shops - it was a Christmas dream village and she'd miss it this year. Though Anastasia and her mother were very different, they had some things in common and Uptown Sparkles was one of them.

She sipped her tea and swallowed the lump in her throat. She glanced out of the window, bit into her toast, and chewed mechanically. A few houses down, Mrs. Sann stood in her nightgown and worn-out slippers. She was outside washing her windows early in the morning fog.

Anastasia leaned forward and licked the shiny butter off her thumb as she watched her neighbour.

Mrs. Sann was rubbing her window vigorously. She was the longest residing resident on Queen's Square North.

She noticed something unusual about her neighbour. She had no coat on and her hands must have been freezing. *Was she upset about something?* She wondered. Why else would she be outside washing her windows so early?

Mrs. Sann tipped the soapy water from the bucket with her heel. She growled, pumped her arms up and down, and kicked the bucket a second time.

Anastasia rushed into the kitchen, grabbed a large container, filled it with hot, soapy water and stepped outside.

"Mrs. Sann?" She hurried over. "Would you like your bucket refilled?"

"Well, bless your heart! Sure." Mrs. Sann picked up her bucket. "How've been holding up?"

"Pretty well. It's a chilly morning. Do you want some help with your windows?"

"Oh, nah. It's only a few windows."

"Okay, I guess I should head back."

Mrs. Sann smiled. "Anastasia, why are you selling your mother's house?"

"I..." She licked her lips. "I would like to keep it but I can't find anyone to manage the building for what I can afford."

Mrs. Sann laughed aloud. "Manage?" She set her fists on her hips. "Your mother never needed a manager."

"Yes, I know, but I'm expected back at work and I have a house in Perth."

Saddened, Mrs. Sann's nodded her head silently and tapped the bucket with the tip of her slipper. "Your mother would be heartbroken if you left."

That stung. She expected it from Mrs. Sann; she'd always been so blunt. Best not go there was her response. "I'm expecting Kirk to meet with me shortly to go over details for the sale. Feel free to stop in for tea later."

"Kirk?"

Watching Mrs. Sann gently nudge the pail, Anastasia recalled when Mrs. Sann's shoes were full of mashed pumpkin on a long-ago Halloween night.

"That boy used to get under my skin."

Mrs. Sann was the sort of person that chased kids up the street back then.

"Do you still get any pumpkin thieves?"

There was Mrs. Sann's smile again. "No, actually," she chortled. "I think either the story or rumour has been permanently set into every generation. I'll always be known as..." She hiccupped. "Mrs. Sann the Wicked Witch of Uptown.

"Eh, you're famous!"

Many years ago, Anastasia and Kirk had laughed in their Halloween costumes with Mrs. Sann's pumpkin in tow, half running and tripping up the street. They disappeared between houses trying to hide.

Baseball bat in hand, Mrs. Sann had chased them across Queen's Square with exceptional speed for her size and age, but lost them in the dark on the cold side of Sydney Street.

"Anastasia!"

Anastasia's hair tickled her sweaty cheek as she peeked beyond the chipped brick corner of Mr. and Mrs. Brown's red brick house.

"She's got her bat," Anastasia panted.

"She's harmless...I think," Kirk giggled. "What if the Browns are home?"

"Don't worry," she assured him. "They're at the pub. I heard my mom talking to Leanne Brown this morning."

As long as they stayed quiet and out of sight, they were safe from Mrs. Sann's wrath.

Anastasia glanced over at Kirk.

He was laughing, closed-mouthed into his vampire cape, with streaks of white watercolour paint dripping down his face. He'd borrowed the paint and penny candy from Dykeman's Hardware store with every intention of putting the can of paint back on the shelf and paying for the candy.

She took one swift glance at Mrs. Sann. There she

was, staring into their direction with venom in her eyes.

She was closing in on them.

Anastasia elbowed Kirk hard in the ribs.

He coughed and dropped his pillowcase full of Halloween goodies.

She bit her lip.

Mrs. Sann swung her baseball bat with a steady arm pointing in their direction.

"Give me *back* my pumpkin!"

The buffoonery was over. Kirk pushed the pumpkin into Anastasia's gut and picked up his pillowcase, shaking like a leaf.

"No way." She handed it back to Kirk. "This was your idea. Don't be a wimp."

"Crap."

She noticed that Kirk often liked to take things that didn't belong to him, but was terrified of getting caught. He was near tears. Of course he was.

"Well?" called Mrs. Sann.

A touch of compassion flickered on Anastasia's face. "First toss aside the bat!"

Mrs. Sann chortled and tapped the end of the bat on the wet pavement near the edge of Mr. and Mrs. Brown's gravel drive, driving home the message.

"This better be the last time you rascals pull a prank like this."

For the second time, Kirk dropped his pillowcase filled with a few apples, an orange, and blessed candy, and took an unsteady step out from behind the brick building, pumpkin cradled in his arms.

Anastasia grabbed him by the cape, took the pumpkin, then pushed her friend into the safety of the house's shadow. She sighed nervously as she walked forward. The Wicked Witch of Uptown stood with a fist on her hip and snorted.

She placed herself and the pumpkin a safe distance from Mrs. Sann. "It's just a pumpkin."

"You think it's funny, don't you?" Mrs. Sann trailed her gaze up and down Anastasia with clear disgust all over her face.

"No."

Straight as a pole in a yellowed bed-sheet costume draped around her skinny body, she stood her ground. She was a fourteen-year-old ghost.

"No? I think you mean, not anymore. Wait 'till I tell your daddy, eh? And your mother, Kirk, I'll be phoning her directly as well."

Anastasia's cheek burned, but she jutted out her chin. She wasn't going to let Mrs. Sann intimidate her and Kirk. Deep down, she knew what her father's involvement would cost her and it suddenly appealed to her feisty, unquenchable spirit to give as much as she was going to get.

"Kirk and me think you're like a beetle rowing across water and up our backs," she pointed her thumb to Kirk behind her.

"We call that the heebie-jeebies," Kirk called out.

"Eh, come here and say that."

"You're all talk," said Anastasia. Mrs. Sann was such a blabbermouth. She loved to threaten kids like Anastasia and Kirk on a regular basis.

"What do you expect? Every year some kid comes and takes my pumpkin. Well, no more."

Anastasia looked over her shoulder. Kirk was now a few feet beside her with two apples in his tight fists.

"It's Halloween. We were just having some fun."

"Willful child." Mrs. Sann sniffed the night air as though she could smell their haughty youth there, then looked at the pumpkin and smiled. "Not a scrap of sense."

She eyed Mrs. Sann's white fingers squeezing the

handle of the bat and sprang forward. Kirk grabbed the edge of the sheet of her costume to hold her back, but tore it. It fluttered in the wind as she kicked the pumpkin.

Crack! It split open, sending strings of gooey innards onto Mrs. Sann's shoes.

Staring at the shoes, she felt very pleased with herself. She snuck a quick glance at Kirk, who looked as delighted as she was. As far as Anastasia was concerned, this was the best part of the evening. Who cares about candy when you get to watch Mrs. Sann blow her horn.

Together, they watched the broken pumpkin roll down the steep street like a flat tire. Tricks did indeed taste better than treats.

A shriek filled Mrs. Sann like a hot air balloon. And then, she blew; long and strong like a foghorn.

Mrs. Sann swung the back of her hand at Anastasia just as Kirk pulled her from harm's way.

Anastasia and Kirk roared, running down the street, past the broken pumpkin, no Halloween candy, and out of Mrs. Sann's sight. All kids knew that Mrs. Sann was the most exciting person to aggravate. She was targeted at Halloween, and her reindeer statue at Christmas would end up painted with black polka dots. She never gave it up. She placed little summer lawn ornaments on her front lawn; they too went missing before summer was over. Mrs. Sann would go house to house looking for her things. No one knew when it all started, but kids were cruel and relentless generation after generation.

Anastasia would pay for it the following day, but for that night, she just wanted to be down at the harbour front, her favourite spot with Kirk, her favourite person. They often sat together on large boulders tossing rocks in the water pretending it was gold and the ocean's secret wishing-well that would grant them their deepest desires.

They wished all sorts of things, like buying the old, decrepit schooner tied to Lloyd's Slip, aiming to restore it one day and sail it around the world. Late at night, they snuck onto the boat and named it Zephyr, then imagined the wind in her crisp, new sails replacing the old, tattered ones while slicing through the Fundy high tide. They took turns being captain and first mate, read books aboard and ate hot dogs and drank lime soda pop. They'd find imaginary treasures, presenting each gift to one another, the next one more extravagant and thoughtful than the last.

Once they finished high school, were going to live out their dream, sail around the world, read, eat seafood, and sip wine from tea cups at every port. The grand plan was to be free of everything the world demanded of them. Instead, they would earn an income by offering trips along the coast. They made a blood-pact promise to live this way. All they would've needed after finishing high school was to save enough to buy and fix Zephyr; Kirk fell in love that summer instead.

"Anastasia, I am so very sorry about how your father reacted the day he left. The day after that terrible Halloween night."

"It's okay. I'm glad he left."

Anastasia checked her watch. 8:45 AM. She winced; she was going to be late.

"Gotta go. Come over for tea later."

"Tomorrow."

"Great, see you then."

Even with their long, tangled history, Kirk was the only realtor Anastasia trusted to sell her mother's home. She heard the soft knock on the door and felt oddly exhilarated. Anastasia swung opened the door.

"Kirk."

He wore an awkward grin on his face.

"Er, I want you to know I'm here to do everything I can to sell your mom's apartment complex. Zero commission."

"Oh, ah. Well, thanks."

This was going to be harder than she thought. Her heart was pounding. "Come in."

Another moment of extraordinarily awkward tension enveloped them. She caught him staring at her sage dress cinched at the waist, which gave her a classic hour-glass figure.

He rubbed the back of his neck. "Thanks. This place still has the same charm."

She laughed. "Yeah."

He echoed her nervous chuckle.

Kirk cleared his throat. "Ah, shall we?"

"Right. Sit down, um..." She pointed to the chesterfield. She took the ottoman adjacent to him.

He opened his briefcase, took out a number of sheets and a pen, then looked up at Anastasia.

She didn't move yet. She sat staring at him.

"Is this a bad time? I can come back another day."

She had an urge to say yes, but it was now or never.

"No." Anastasia got up and walked along the library shelves, hand tracing the bounded backs.

She took the letter off the shelf and handed it to him. He opened it, his jaw dropped, and his eyes watered.

"How To Restore The Sailboat of Your Dreams," she sniffed.

"Annie."

The tension in the room rose to the degree of volcanic eruption. She looked at him familiarly, and she saw Kirk's old anchoring eyes again.

He sat, not moving an inch.

She pulled the book off the shelf, opened it, casually flipped through some of the pages, and stopped at page 354.

"...and, when she sails sweetly," she choked and looked directly at him, "...you're transported to a place from before trouble was trouble, and time was time."

Her eyes gleamed as she looked at the sailboat, just like the one they were supposed to restore. She turned her face to the bookshelves, wiped a few tears.

"Anastasia?"

She turned. "Ha, who'd ever think you'd turned your back on me and then later help me sell my mother's house through my father's real estate company."

Kirk's expression was written all over his face.

"How is Daddy, by the way?"

Kirk's lips parted.

"You could have waited, Kirk. We could have figured things out...Did you really love Cassandra?"

Kirk swallowed hard. "I -"

"You what?" She cut him off. "You what, Kirk? Forgot your promise to me?"

"No, I didn't." He lifted a hand, gesturing for a chance to speak, but didn't know what else to say.

"Why didn't you wait?"

"How long have you known that we weren't half siblings?"

"What does it matter, Kirk? You were practically married before I got home."

He swiftly retrieved the pen and papers and walked to the door.

"I'm sorry...I got-"

"Right. Got to leave." She stood up and ushered him to the door. "Go ahead, this is what you do best. You check out every time you're in the wrong, or never ready to face the truth. Or...or be a real man!"

Kirk reached for the doorknob and paused.

"Go!"

She closed the door behind him.

He pleaded with her from the other side of the door, "now is not the time, but I will explain, if you'll let me!"

Against the door, she sobbed with an air of tragic relinquishment.

"Please?"

Instinctively, she ran up to her old room. It had been turned into a sewing room, but it still had her old brown teddy bear atop hat boxes and a few pictures from school. One of her and Kirk, wearing Halloween costumes, was still resting on her old bureau. It was the last time either of them went trick or treating at the age of fourteen- the ghost and the vampire.

They looked so happy and carefree. She touched the frame.

She decided to get some air. A walk might clear her thoughts. The sun high up in the sky now burned brightly through the fog that started off most days in Saint John.

Now she finally knew the real reason why her

parents got separated: they both cheated on each other. The one and only time she asked her mother what had happened, Bethany had burst into tears. She assumed it was her father's fault and she was right.

She remembered that fateful winter day, the day he left and never came back. She was outside with him as he packed his things. This was likely the last time she'd ever see him around. Every kid heard similar stories at school. Losing one parent was expected.

She stood up, walked to the street side of his purple van, leaned her forehead against the driver's side door, and stretched her arms across, hugging it, as though to never let him go. She wanted him to hug her too, fiercely. Tears ran down her young ruddy cheeks as she traced a square on the side of her father's dust-caked van. She wrote the letter, 'I' with the tip of her finger, remembering how her father had traced a little phrase on her back when she was sick. She didn't want to say goodbye to the tenderness her father so often gave her. A piece of gravel caught her eye, and she picked it up. She glanced from the stone to the van. Her heart was pounding; she knew what she was going to do. She lifted the sharp piece and marked into the side of the van like a fork being dragged along an old school chalkboard: 'I Love You Dadd'. Between her fingers she held her writing tool in the air, for a moment feeling in the wrong but resolute about leaving him something he wouldn't forget. He'd never forget her. She scratched one line of the last letter, 'y', just as her father hurried to her side. His red, swollen eyes blinked in disbelief.

Overcome with fear and shame, she dropped the gravel. He threw a stuffed duffle bag inside and left the van door opened.

Her lips twitched and her chin trembled.

He held his keys tightly in his fist and slugged her between the upper lip and nose.

Gasping for breath she heard the van rev and smelled the exhaust. Copious amounts of blood poured out from her face flooding her eyes, nostrils, and mouth. She coughed, spat blood from her mouth and blinked the red fog blurring her vision. She marked him, and he marked her, for life.

It took weeks for the deep flesh wound to heal while she waited for plastic surgery. Her face healed leaving a slight disfigurement above her cupid's bow but it was her nose that told her sad story.

And now what? She tossed Kirk out. She'd have to call a new company and start fresh, again.

Brand new tears formed in the corners and valleys of her eyes as she fought to keep them at bay. She turned left on Adelaide to avoid staring eyes. She stopped at the café on King Street and called Mr. Fogart's assistant, Marley.

Marley wasn't picking up her phone and after two cappuccinos Anastasia decided to walk into Fogart Realty's office. Mr. Fogart was in the middle of a meeting with his employees, including Kirk. She stood there unblinkingly, not saying a word.

Mr. Fogart rose from his seat, told everyone to stay put until he returned, and left the boardroom with his white cane, leading Anastasia to his personal office, where he closed the door and asked her to have a seat, if she would.

She stood there, and asked him many questions, including what took him so long. He tried to explain but she wasn't satisfied. She walked out past his employees and Kirk followed her to Main Street. The cold, salty wind whipped her red curls around. He asked her if she was going to be okay.

She broke down in his arms. Once she had composed herself enough to talk, she told him he was the only one she wanted to sell her mother's home.

He agreed, but he did something more. He pulled her close to him, like he used to and rubbed the valley between her knuckles. His voice turned soft, as he told her he never wanted to hurt her, and that Cassandra picked him up when his heart was broken for her.

She blurted out that Mr. Fogart was her biological father. He cursed and told her that he and Cassandra separated three years ago, and that he had partial custody of his child. He smiled and kissed her hand. "You know I loved you then and still do."

Long minutes transpired as people walked by. Some gestured at Kirk to kiss her.

Another, "What are you waiting for, the sun to shine, everyone Uptown gets kissed in the fog, so go on."

They were blushing but held fast. Finally, they were alone.

"So, you're the wharf master's daughter?"

Anastasia's straightened her back, took a step closer, and caressed Kirk's messy hair in the muggy, grey morning, and whispered, "and so, you're the stone carver's son, eh?"

Kirk swung her around. "Yeah."

A little old lady pulled a beautiful red carnation from her bouquet and gave it to Kirk saying, "Give this to the love of your life, honey - trust me, moments like these don't wash up on the Bay of Fundy every day."

Kirk took the flower and nodded a thank you.

He kissed Anastasia.

Kirk whispered in Anastasia's ear. "You're the ocean's deepest, most precious secret etched in my soul.” He touched her cheek and caressed it. “And I am your ship.”

Anastasia pulled Kirk close and kissed his warm lips. “Let’s get ready to sail then, eh.”

Amanda Evans

Fresh Baked History

The bell above the bakery door chimed, the breeze that accompanied the dark dressed man blew the delightful scents of her trade back into the baker's face.

“Can I help you?” she asked when he walked past the two tables of cookies piled high without looking at them.

“Is Andy Melson here?” he asked. His voice was clipped and his words hurried. Easy signs he wasn't a Maritimer.

“Andrea Melson,” she corrected. “I go by Andy.”

“Is there somewhere we can go to talk?” he asked, only surprised for a moment that the person he was looking for wasn't the person he thought he was looking for.

“Right here seems fine. If you don't mind the crowd.” An amused grin split her face. She had a lovely smile. The stranger turned at her words to survey the empty room he'd just walked through. His lips drew into an even flatter line. She worked to keep her laughter back, not wanting to offend a potential customer, even an out-of-towner. Truth was, the bakery was only busy three times during the day: when they first opened and the regulars came in with standing orders, at lunch when people from schools and offices came in to buy their lunch, and just before they closed when the penny-pinchers came to barter for the unsold products.

"The issue is of a rather sensitive nature," the suit responded, though his tone remained flat.

"And who did you say you are again?" she asked, knowing he hadn't yet introduced himself.

"Erick Ikerverson," he replied. "I'm a lawyer for Myers, Craft & Stein."

"I don't know that company," Andy replied after a few moments. She didn't know all the law firms in the city, but that one didn't sound local. She kept a good-natured smile on her face but it was a little more forced.

"It's a law firm in New Hampshire," he told her, taking a card from the case he pulled from his suit pocket. She took it and studied it for a moment. "I represent Mrs.Livingstone."

"That old bird?" she blurted, then blushed. The heat burned the politeness away, leaving the face of a serious businesswoman behind.

A twitch gripped the corner of his mouth pulling it into a hint of a smile. "I apologize, I represent the estate of Mr. and Mrs. Harold Livingstone." He corrected himself.

"Sally!" Andy called, her voice echoing in

the flour-filled air. “I'm going to be in the office for a bit,” she told the worker in the back.

There was a shuffling of feet and the larger, older Sally came through the doorway. Dusty hands braced on apron clad hips. Immediately Andy looked younger. It was easy to tell the dullness of her skin and clothes was the result of the fine flour rather than age.

“Lunch came early today?” the older woman asked, her eyes never leaving the younger man in the suit, and there was a hunger that said she could eat him up whole without a problem.

“Something like that,” Andy agreed, a small smile on her lips at the way Sally's gaze made the man swallow a few times. “Right this way Mr. Erickson.” Andy gestured to the doorway that Sally was guarding like a wild thing.

“Ikerverson,” he corrected, hustling by Sally, whose grin grew as she watched him move.

The office, just off the kitchen, was small and polluted with papers. A baker’s dozen worth of trees had given their lives for this mess. Andy took her seat behind the desk and brushed some of the papers to the side to find the notepad below.

The lawyer took a seat on the other side of the desk and put his case on the floor, loathe to have his papers mingle with hers. “So what's this about the old bi... uh, Mrs. Livingstone?" she prompted.

"Mrs. Livingstone passed away six days ago," he opened.

"So the rumors were true." She didn't seem shocked or concerned, just a woman storing away information. "How does this affect me?"

"You were mentioned in her will," he told her.

Now she looked shocked, her green eyes growing. "Me? Why? How? I barely knew her."

"It happens." Erick shrugged his well-dressed shoulders.

The room stayed silent for a few moments. "Are you going to tell me what it said?" she asked, her eyes shrinking just a little.

He grabbed his case, pulled it up onto his lap, and opened it. He pulled out a single sheaf of paper, which he dutifully passed over. Andy's brows cocked as she looked at it. It didn't look like a will. It looked like a ransom letter. A plain white page with a few lines neatly typed on it. There was an embossed image on the paper. The exact same water mark as on his business card.

"This is not the official will," Erick stated. "At the request of the other parties involved, they wanted your information to exclude any details not relevant to you. If you wish to fight their decision, we can make the request."

Her eyes lifted off the page when he said that. There was no indication in his tone about what would make the most amount of sense. She shrugged. If the rest of the information didn't pertain to her, then there was no reason other than simple curiosity to fight their request. She let it slide.

"It feels like some kind of joke," she told him in all seriousness, her eyes meeting his. Her green eyes met his brown. Her pistachio to his chocolate, his earth to her grass.

"I assure you, it is not," he told her in a calm voice, but the words held a strange accent. If she had to guess, he was a second generation American. "Did you want me to bring in the local authorities to prove its validity?"

She considered it for only a moment. Someone she recognized, at least by reputation, would help, but they were a small bakery, advertised through word of mouth. Gossip and chin-wagging of an official police visit could be harmful. Her eyes dropped to the page again.

> *To Andy Melson, the baker: I am giving you the first inspection of my property. I trust Andy to go through everything within the house, and all of mine and Harold's possessions, to determine what and where any of my non-monetary assets would best be*

delivered to help enrich the city of Saint John.

"Not very forthcoming with the details, was she?" Andy asked, having read the scant words through a few more times.

"Not at all," his face crinkled in a grin, "but you'll understand when you see what's in the house."

"You could just tell me," she put the words out there.

"I couldn't do it justice," he replied. The grin shifted to a true smile that formed around his words, making his New England accent more noticeable.

Andy sighed and rolled her eyes. "And when do I get to see this stuff?" Her words held nothing but irritation, but her soul was ratcheting up with curiosity.

"We could go now," he offered, closing his case and shuffling to stand.

"I have work to do," she replied tartly. "I can't just take off on a whim."

"You said you close at three?" he asked, a frown pulling his lips flat again.

"I didn't, but our sign did," she corrected him, agreeing with him at the same time.

“I can come back then,” he offered, and she could see he was trying to bring the reassuring smile back on his face. It wasn't working.

“Uh. No,” she shut him down again. “I'll meet you there, around 5:30?” she suggested, hoping to put him on the spot by choosing such a busy time.

“Do you know which house it is?” he asked.

“The old one on Waterloo, by Agar place,” she replied without thinking about it.

"That doesn't really narrow it down...” he let the words he was going to add die unspoken.

“It does to the folk from around here,” she snapped. “I'll see you there around 5:30.” She concluded the conversation, standing before he could say anything else to throw a wrench into her day.

“Are you allergic to dust?” he asked, climbing to his feet to match her.

“Dust?” she asked, dumbfounded at the sudden change in topic. “No...” The word dragged itself out through a layer of uncertainty.

“Good. The cleaners have been in briefly, but until you've done your evaluation, there's not much they can do.” He struck out a hand, and she took it. “Wear something you don't mind getting dirty.”

Her eyebrows rose again as she took in the suit that he was wearing and his tidy appearance compared to her jeans and apron. “I'll take that under advisement. Thank you.” She stepped past him to open the office door, unable to miss the sound of Sally scrambling away from her eavesdropping.

She stepped into the imperceptibly warmer kitchen and breathed in the flour-filled, lawyer-free air. “Thank you, Mr. Ikerverson,” she said as he passed by her.

The well-dressed lawyer nodded and hurried past the counter, giving Sally, the guardian, a wide berth. “Heading away so quickly, mister?” Sally called, catching his attention. “Sure you don't want to take something here home with you?” Her eyebrows waggled at him.

“Uh... no. Thank you. I'm fine.” Erick said from the other side of the counter. Even without seeing her expression, he could feel her intent.

“Yes, yes, you are," Sally agreed salaciously under her breath. As he reached the door, she called out, "Have a good day, Mr. Ikerverson.”

“Yes. You too,” he replied and then the chime above the door told them he was gone.

“Sally, you're awful,” she said with a smile to the older woman.

Sally smiled back and shrugged, "You miss 100% of the shots you don't take."

Andy said nothing, just looked up at the clock over the door, surprised that it hadn't even been 10 minutes since he'd walked in. It felt like forever and judging by the cat-that-ate-the-canary look that Sally was sporting, that was how long she was going to hear about it.

It was just shy of six when he finally arrived, looking over his shoulder and completely uncertain of himself. He looked good in a pair of washed out jeans that hugged him tight from hips to knee and then hung loose the rest of the way down his legs, a pair of old sneakers coated in dirt, and a gray t-shirt that used to have a band name advertised on it, now faded, peaked out of an unzipped black coat. The only thing remaining of the uppity lawyer was the hair and his soft looking, well-groomed hands.

Andy's own yoga pants, crocs, and ponytail still won for the most casual. "Is it okay to park my car there?" he asked, gesturing with a thumb at the Service NB parking lot.

"Is it yours or a rental?" she asked with a wicked smile.

"A rental," he stated slowly, his face falling, lips forming an uncertain line.

“NB plates should be fine. The regulars won’t bother it," she told him calmly. "You didn't leave anything valuable where it could be seen did you?”

He paused and mentally brought up an inventory of what was in the car and where. Nothing visible. “What I meant was will I get a fine? What about the locals?”

The look on her face changed in proportion to his worry, going from amused to wicked. “Waterloo has a reputation.” She didn't divulge on the fact that it was a street of saints and sinners. Three churches, a methadone clinic, high traffic prostitution, two homeless shelters, and a Tim's. You had to live here to get it.

“I'm going to move the car,” he told her.

“Where to?” she asked, swiveling to take in the fully saturated curb side.

“New Hampshire,” he muttered.

She chuckled, a warm, genuine laugh. “Oh, come on, it'll be fine,” she told him, flicking her hand like swatting away a fly and putting enough emphasis to make her words ring true by force of will alone.

“Besides, how long can this take?”

Now it was his turn to give her a look. A ghost of a smile climbed up one side of his face and he turned to the gate. There had always been a gate, hip high and extended across the front of the lot. It hadn't blocked the driveway until recently. After the first window was broken Mrs. Livingstone added an extra gate to the front, afraid of sleeping alone. It was a cold metal meshing that went from the corner of one house to the other, blocking the danger from reaching her. Erick pulled a jumble of keys from his pocket; Andy could see that they were boring. No key-chains, no fob, no cheeky plastic forms over the top of the dull metal keys. On his third try, he unlocked the gate and gestured for her to proceed him into the tiny, postage stamp lawn.

She stepped through and took in the house while he locked the gate. It was an old house, and it was obvious that it had been built long before it's neighbors, with their flat, boring cookie-cutter shape and straight unimaginative lines. They were built during a population boom, when cheap and fast trumped personality or individuality, and the word architecture was a curse, not a description. The neighbouring houses grew huge and hulking around the little gem. If it had been a flower, it would have died in their shadow, but the little house now looked more impressive by comparison.

The sides were done with a slate gray wooden shingle, and the trim in curling bold designs that Andy could only describe as 'Gothic'. It was painted a cream color or had aged to the color of buttercream. Windows of different sizes were speckled around. Sharp, sloped roofs, and a widow's watch completed the look. She had no way to date the building; it wasn't her expertise, but she wouldn't be surprised to learn it was one of the first buildings in the city.

"Coming?" Erick asked, holding the door open and breaking the illusion of grandeur. She could see the rickety stairs that led to a sagging stoop, missing shingles and boarded up windows.

"Coming," she replied, though it wasn't necessary as she was already starting up the few steps.

"Be careful," he warned as the last step rocked under her. She glared but didn't say anything.

The inside of the house was... that was as far as she could easily describe it. Cluttered, almost artfully chaotic. Those were good words to start describing it, but they didn't really paint the picture. She looked over at Erick, a smirk on his face and a shrug in his shoulders. His eyes snapped saucily with the unsaid 'told you'.

"The boxes have already come up from the basement, anything damaged or moldy was thrown away," he told her, explaining away a good amount of the clutter.

"You've already been through the boxes?" she asked.

"Nope," he said, looking straight into her eyes. "That's your job. We just got rid of the stuff that couldn't be salvaged."

"And if I don't want the job?" she asked stiffly, not liking his tone or smugness.

"Then you sign the paperwork. I've got it back in my car and we let the family in Singapore know they can start the bulldozing."

Andy's jaw dropped in confusion. "Singapore, bulldozing?"

Erick turned on the lights and closed the door he'd been standing in front of. The glow was soft, but it illuminated better than the light from the outside. It filled the corners that the natural light coming through the window just couldn't touch. She was almost let down that it was a regular overhead light and not something more extravagant.

"Sit?" Erick asked, leading the two of them into the parlor.He walked with his shoes on and she followed his example. Tracks of shoe prints ghosted on the hardwood floor; many feet had been in here recently, though none had stepped on any of the rugs. Andy avoided them as well.

The chair that Erick took was a deep comfortable affair of sandy brown covering that would be hard pressed to go out of style. Andy sat in the middle of the couch across from him, so close to the edge of the cushions that she was barely on it at all.

"The Livingstones had no children," Erick stated,

the obvious when he saw that she wasn't going to make herself more comfortable.

“His brother’s family are their only living relatives. His brother married a woman in Singapore. He's been there for the last 35 years. He has three children and seven grandchildren, and they are the ones that will inherit it all," he told her and she nodded.

"They have already stated that they have no intentions of moving to Saint John. They're only coming into Canada long enough to sign the paperwork. They don't want anything to do with this windfall other than the money.” His words were neither judging nor praising their decision. He had no dog in this race; this wasn't his home.

“Joyceline knew all of this, but they are the only family she had left to give it to. She and her husband loved Saint John, they had since the day they first came here and they didn't want all of the history of their life thrown away when it could help the city, even if only a little bit.” Andy nodded following the path his mind treaded earlier. “If the will did not specifically give you first rights to this place, they would have already sold it, lock, stock, and barrel before her corpse even had a chance to cool.”

“Ah,” the sound leaped to her mouth, surprised that he'd displayed any opinion. “Why not just donate everything?” she asked.

"Where?" It was a simple question, but a loaded one as well.

"The museum?" It was a question as much as a suggestion, she had no faith that it was the right answer.

"The clothes? The T.V.? The books?" he countered.

"A pawn shop?"

"That doesn't help Saint John," he countered again. "The stuff has to be sorted, and they chose you to do it." He shrugged, then leaned forward slightly, like they were sharing a secret, and perhaps they were. "Between you and me," he said softly, "I don't really want to give anyone that has never stepped foot in the city any more than I have to."

She smiled at him conspiratorially. "I'll do my best," she told him without realizing that she was agreeing to the job. "But why me? Is there any word in the will about it?"

"None," he told her. She frowned, pulling her bottom lip into her mouth and sucking on it for a moment. She'd hoped that there was a reason for the old woman's choice. She let out a pent-up sigh and coughed slightly as the dust went where it would. Flipping over her wrist, she looked at the watch. 7:15 PM already. The time had flown. She had about an hour, possibly two, before she had to get home. Work started early at a bakery.

"Let's get started!" she said with a newborn determination.

"How can I help?" Erick asked, standing as well.

"You're going to get your hands dirty?" she mock gasped, raising a hand to cover her loosely swinging jaw.

"Ha, ha," he countered, but his eyes twinkled, transforming them from dirt brown to chocolate. "I have to be here anyway, at least until the family arrives and signs off the paperwork. I may as well help." He shrugged; he didn't want to appear too eager.

Her eyebrows quirked, like she'd caught his curiosity coming to the fore. "Do we have any unused boxes, or paper for wrapping stuff? What about markers and tape?"

"Uh... no. Well, maybe tape," he replied after a pause.

She blew out a breath, pushing her loose bangs around like gauzy curtains. "We'll make do," she said and brightened. "Let's start with the boxes," she stated, looking at the towering piles that were all around the room and in the entry hallway. "You can bring them over here and put them on the couch."

The first hour, and then the second flew by, the dust coming off the neatly folded and taped boxes in dancing, cough-inducing clouds that eventually settled on them, claiming the couple as their own.

“Kleenex?” Erick asked when Andy started coughing until the tears streamed down her face.

“Thank you,” Andy gasped, accepting the wilting white square. She wiped the gritty tears away and wadded up the Kleenex, shoving it into her pocket.

“Oh! Wow! Goodness! It's almost 10!” she exclaimed the words like they were four separate thoughts. “I've gotta get home.” She started casting around for her coat.

“It's 9:38.” He told her.

“I have to be up by 3:00 AM,” she told him, finally remembering that she hadn't brought one. “Tomorrow?”

“Tomorrow,” he agreed, grabbing his own coat and following behind her, shutting off the lights. “We'll have to push hard to try to get everything done by the twelfth.”

Andy jerked to a stop. “The twelfth? That's like...” she paused to remember the date. “Four days away,” she finally stated, dumbstruck “Why the twelfth?”

“That's when the family will be arriving to sign the documents.”

Her shoulders sank. The pile of boxes had hardly dwindled in the better part of three hours and that was just the tip of the cookie.

"Do you..." he started to make a suggestion, but she drew her breath and squared her shoulders, bracing herself for the powerful sigh she let out. In three hours they found some warm clothes for the Coats for Kids group, regular clothes for the St. Vincent de Paul Society, the older and more unique clothes were in a pile to be donated to the Saint John Theater Company. There was another pile ready to be wrapped donated to the museum. Sure, they'd found some stuff the family could auction off but the city was benefiting more.

"We can start earlier tomorrow," she stated as they stepped together into the chilly yard.

There was a click of the key making the tumblers align. "What time?" he asked.

"How's 4:30 PM?"She asked, crossing the black grass in two strides and then waiting for him to unlock the gate.

He only took a moment to cross the yard and step beside her. He stood close enough that she could feel the warmth radiating from him on her bare arms. "4:30," he agreed, letting them out. He swung the barrier open and stuck his hand out towards Andy. "Nice working with you, Mrs. Melson."

“Andy,” she corrected him, taking his grimy hand.

“Andy,” he repeated, as if it would be difficult to commit it to memory.

“It was fun getting you dirty, too, Erick.” she replied saucily using his first name. The dimness took the expression from his face, but the grip on her hand was firm as he pumped it more times than was necessary. She didn't mind. There was a strength in his hands that she hadn't expected, and it was a well-known fact that you could tell a lot about a guy from the way he shook your hand. This handshake told her it would not be hard at all to like him. He eventually broke the grip to turn and lock the gate. When he was done, she was gone from sight.

The next day, Andy was waiting at the gate 15 minutes early. Her car was parked snugly against the curb and brimming with boxes, tape, paper, markers, bags, gloves, and everything else they could need. Ten minutes later, Erick arrived.

“How was the car last night?” she asked him with a mischievous look.

“Left alone,” he said with a smile on his face. “That's why I felt okay leaving it there again today. Ready?”

“Yep, I just need some help bringing this stuff inside,” she told him, a hitched thumb pointing at the car.

His eyes widened. “Sure,” he agreed, moving to unlock the gate. Andy moved toward the car and dug out the supplies. The gate and door were both gaping open for her when she started in that direction. The hall and parlor they'd been working in the previous night was filled with empty boxes all put together and waiting, and on the table was a box filled similar to the one she was carrying.

“Great minds think alike,” he said when he nudged past her to drop off the box of boxes he was carrying.

“And fools seldom differ,” she countered automatically, then put her box to join its mate on the table before heading back out. “It's a good thing; we're going to need lots,” she commented as they made their way back to the car. “Let’s just hope we don't run out of space.”

“That shouldn't be an issue. I'll take the filled boxes to their destinations as long as you label them properly,” he told her.

“Me label them? Why not you?”

“I have horrible writing! Everyone tells me I should have been a doctor, not a lawyer,” he said with a laugh, grabbing the next box.

“What makes you think I'm any better?” she asked, grabbing her own.

"I've seen the writing on the signs at the bakery, also the way the cookies were decorated bode well for a steady hand," he reminded her.

"That could have been Sally," she told him.

"Not cougar enough," he responded with a smile that she could hear but was hidden behind the boxes he was carrying.

She laughed and would have smacked him if they both didn't have their hands full. It took three trips each to unload the car and entomb themselves in the house.

Conversation between the two of them was easy, and they quickly found a rhythm. When they stopped for a break a few hours in, Andy could only stare, amazed at the amount of boxes all taped up and marked for delivery. There were so many charities to be found in a city when a person was actively trying to find them.

The hours melted away. They finished the basement boxes and a few of the rooms on the main floor. Erick kept meticulous records as to where any item of note or worth was being donated to and why. They were about to start another room when Erick's rumbling stomach could no longer be ignored.

"Supper?" Erick asked around 8:30 PM.

"I should get going. I have some stuff to catch up on at home," she replied, dusting her hand on her dirty pants. "You're sure you know where you're taking this stuff?"

"It's written out, and I'm sure I can look it up if I have to," he replied. "Same time tomorrow?"

"Sounds good," she agreed, heading towards the door. She was gone by the time he finished taping the last few boxes.

She was standing outside the gate, dressed in baggy, candy-pink pants that looked more like pajamas than day pants, and a short-sleeved top with a picture of a sucker on it that said *Lick my Lollipop* in glittery letters.

"Happy Friday!" she called when he jogged into view. "I brought food," she added, holding up a large brown bag.

"Wow, great!" he yelped, a sudden hunger rumbled through his stomach that she could hear. He'd been on the move so much that the thought of eating hadn't even crossed his mind.

"I guess that answers the now or later question," she stated with a twist of a smile that said that she was laughing with him, not at him. He unlocked the gate, letting her through. She walked on ahead and sat on the small stoop, stretching her legs out. Erick sat beside her and felt the slight damp from an earlier rain that hadn't dried. He rolled his eyes and accepted it as one of those days.

"What have ya got?" he asked.

"Leftovers from the bakery," she replied, taking some sandwiches and cookies out, then dove in again for the two bottles of water. "We're closed on the weekends."

"Thanks," he said, helping himself to the pile.

Side by side, they ate. Side by side they worked and side by side they passed the evening, going from room to room. Some were quick and easy, like the kitchen; others not nearly as quick; and some were completely awkward and intrusive. By the time they were battling yawns, the bottom two floors were done.

"Did you want to take a look in the attic tonight, or wait until tomorrow?" Erick asked when she put the last box in the pile reserved for the Saint John Library.

Andy stood and leaned back, her hands braced on her hips as she stretched muscles that had cramped from so much bending over. She quirked her lips to the side and sucked on the inside of her cheek; the curiosity was eating at her, especially with the amused look on his face, but she tamped it down.

"Tomorrow," she stated decisively. "Let's end tonight on a high note."

"Agreed," he laughed, stretching his back as well and rotating his shoulders. His arms felt like limp noodles. No matter how many hours you worked out, when push came to shove, using the muscles to actually do something always made them feel limp. “Same time tomorrow?”

“Did you want to start earlier?” she asked.

“Sure,” he blurted out.“So long as there isn't someone at home upset at how much time we're spending together,” he added with an awkward laugh.

She laughed at his blush, but there was a pink stain creeping up her neck as well. “It'll be fine. I don't think Percy will mind too much.”

“Percy?”

“My cat,” she laughed at the look of shock on his face. He shook his head upon hearing about her pet.

“Noon then?”

“Noon,” she agreed. She would have suggested earlier, but she didn't think the lawyer knew what 6 AM was.

Eleven o’clock found a shocked baker standing in front of the house, cradling a cup of coffee from Timmies and staring at the cloud of dust being swept out the door. “Erick?” Andy called, letting herself into the yard through the unlocked gate.

Erick was dancing with the broom, earphone in,

and dressed in the same outfit as the first night. He was bleating badly off-key along with the music from his phone that no one else could hear. The pile of boxes from the previous night were mostly gone, and what wasn't, was piled neatly in rows in the parlor.

Watching the strange man dance, she was tempted to knock the broom away and to slip into his arms to be his partner. He jumped and let out a startled "Eep!" seeing her watching him.

"But I won't do that!" she finished the song for him, singing equally off-key.

"Meatloaf fan?" he asked, leaning the broom against the wall and standing straighter.

"Isn't everyone?" she replied with full seriousness.

"Hungry? I brought muffins," he told her, pointing to the clear plastic bag on the table with the unmistakable Tim Horton's box inside it.

"Later," she said holding up her cup.

"Ready to go upstairs?" he asked with a grin reminiscent of a cat that ate the canary.

"After you," she gestured. He nodded and started up the stairs with her close on his heels. They got to the second floor and Erick led the way to the third doorway on the right. Andy had originally thought it was a closet until she opened the door the night before and saw a staircase hidden out of sight.

Today, he threw open the door and started up the stairs. They weren't carpeted, but they did have a fairly thick tread on them.

They climbed up, 35 stairs exactly. Andy counted them to keep from pushing past him and to keep her eyes in respectable areas. The attic was mind numbing. If Erick hadn't grabbed her cup, she would have dropped it.

"What the..." There were no more words in her at the moment.

The entire floor was open and lined with shelves; even the pillars that kept the roof up were lined with shelves. Between two such pillars was a thin set of stairs that angled up to meet the wall right between the windows. These stairs, she knew, led to the widow's watch. She walked forward and saw two tables, each larger than a teacher's desk. On one sat a sewing machine and paints, and the other had wood working tools.

It would have been an impressive library if the shelves held books, but they didn't. Andy moved closer to the shelves and her eyes widened further. They were filled with dolls. Hand made dolls. Hundreds of them. Each and every one of them was painted and dressed in precisely made clothing. Each doll stood on its own, or was supported by a metal frame, and below each doll was a sketch or a picture. She moved around the room. They were all Saint

John residents. She stopped at Elsie Wayne. Elsie had been a well-loved mayor and the picture under her was the cover of her book. Andy carefully pried the image from the shelf and flipped it over.

Elsie Wayne

Elsie was mayor of Saint John. In 1977 she was elected to the city council and in 1983 she was voted mayor. She was the first woman female and as far as we are concerned she will always be the best.

Elsie reminds us of Molasses Cookies

The recipe filled the rest of the page. Confused, Andy put the image back. The doll next to Elsie's was a balding man with a rather large paunch and a set of hard, drunken eyes. She took the photo, a Polaroid, and flipped it over.

Bald man of Waterloo Street.

We call him Mack.

We don't think he's very nice. He is out late and never with the same woman. We haven't seen him beat anyone yet, but we worry.

The bald man of Waterloo Street reminds us of Chow Chow.

There was no rhyme or reason to the dolls. There were famous people like Donald Sutherland (Down East Lobster Stew), Walter Pidgeon (Beer Potato

Soup), Stompin' Tom Connors (Acadian Buttermilk Pie), and Lyman Ward (Fiddlehead Omelet), and politicians Myra Freeman (Cod Cakes), George Edward King (Cabbage Rolls), and Joseph Medill (Tartar Sauce), but they were outnumbered by the regular folk.

"What is all this?" she finally managed to ask after looking at perhaps a dozen of them.

"It was their hobby," he replied with a shrug. "I didn't know what to think when I saw it either. It honestly creeped me out," he admitted, then walked to a doll not far past where she stood. "Look at this one," he pointed. It was a young girl heavily made up and wearing something completely inappropriate. "They didn't pull any punches."

The photo called her Sally, and the writing said: *I think Sally is just a poor, sweet child doing what she has to, to get by.* The recipe was cherry jubilee cookies.

"If you come here," he said and moved to another shelf, "I think this is when Harold passed away." She joined him. "You can see in the next dozen or so dolls where she tries a number of different ways of making the bodies before things smoothed out again."

She looked and easily saw what he was talking about. For an entire shelf the dolls looked different. There were cloth bodies, apple faced stick bodies, clay, and even ones made with knock-off barbie dolls. “How long have you spent in here?” she asked.

“The entire first day,” he admitted. “It's a history tour, journal, commentary of the city life, and cook book all in one.”

“It's surreal,” she told him.

“Are you ready for the last room?” he asked, ignoring her words.

“There's more?” Her heart picked up at the thought of what more the house and the strange old lady still had to give.

Erick started up the little stairway first and pushed the hatch open. Then he moved to the side and let Andy brush past. It was a tight fit and, for a moment, they were pressed close. Heated skin touching, folded cloth catching as she moved past him. Erick slowly let his breath out.

The tiny glass room was odd, to say the least. From hips down, the small landing was still attic, from waist up it was all windows. It had an all around a view that at one time must have been glorious, but now, due to its taller brothers, was hooded on three sides. The last side looked down on Waterloo Street. There was a stiff-backed but comfortable chair. The wall that connected the attic to the widow watch was a shelf piled high with journals, sketch books, and Polaroid cameras.

Erick knew the moment she found it. There was a sharp intake of breath, a hitched breath out, and the sound of movement. She came down the stairs, Polaroid clutched in her hand so hard she risked permanently ruining it.

“It's me!” she exclaimed, thrusting it at him as if it was all his fault. It wasn't a bad picture of her .She was just carrying a tray of bread into the racks in the shop. Andy couldn't pinpoint any exact moment that it was taken - it was a common enough scene at the bakery - but it still made her feel vulnerable.

“Did you see the back?” He asked softly, not knowing really what he could say. He'd debated taking the picture out all together, unsure how she would react when she saw it, but it was all the explanation he'd yet to find as to why Joyceline Livingstone had chosen Andrea in the first place.

She started to say something, then stopped, dragged in a few deep breaths and let them out slowly. She blinked twice, unfurled her angry death grip on the photo, and flipped it over.

Andrea Melanson.

I like the girl from the bakery. She reminds me of bread. You can always trust a person that reminds you of bread.

G. Abrams

G. Abrams is a writer and musician who currently resides in Saint John, NB with his three sons: Alexander, Zakkary, and Mason. He is an eclectic writer who draws inspiration from across the literary spectrum, from H. P. Lovecraft to Margaret Atwood. His short story, “Rot” is his debuting published work as an up-and-coming author.

Rot

It always appeared that his words fell on deaf ears, and his actions seemingly met with disregard. Yet she smiled and laughed and played with him as if her blackened heart had a seam: a seam in which a crack might one day allow something he did to penetrate its hardened crust. That had always been enough for him.

Emily Jane was the object of his affection. She was a sad girl who hid behind a smiling mask. He saw through this act - at least, he'd always told himself he did. He wrote her poetry, sang her songs, took her to movies, and bought her trinkets that reminded him of her. She was, to him, almost a Dickensian character, as though she was a product of Mrs. Havisham's tutelage. His very own Estella. He told himself he would be able to undo the spell this wicked, jilted witch had thrown upon her. She always stayed the same though: closed off like a dusty book on a shelf, perhaps waiting for the right person to open her up and read her dark story. He knew deep in his soul that he would be the one to finally crack that spine.

She almost never said no to a date with him. They had met once a week for the last 6 months. A big accomplishment, for him, as their dates had been sparse up until this point- maybe once a month if he had hounded her enough. He took the fact that she made time for him more readily now as a sign of headway towards discovering her secrets. Romantic walks along Harbour Passage, ice cream at the Pumpkin Patch, and late night rock shows at Peppers Pub; each date was meticulously thought out to try and elicit some form of emotion from this wounded bird that he intended to mend. He cherished every moment with her, even though things never went the way he had envisioned them. His grand romantic gestures were supposed to stoke some internal fire that he imagined burned with the same desire he felt for her. Instead, she laughed and smiled each time he attempted to kiss her.

"I'm waiting for the right moment," he recalled her remarking one time. Something was different about Emily Jane.

Sometimes that smiling mask slipped from her face, revealing a blank stare where she seemed to get lost within her own thoughts, sliding into another world where he was invisible to her. She would mumble nonsense under her breath, repetitive words he never could quite make out. He thought of it as one of those quirks that made Emily Jane so unique. After each of these odd spells resolved, she would look at him, fix her face back to that goofy smile, and lick her lips. The puzzlement he felt towards her and her mysterious trances melted away each time she licked those lips. He envisioned himself as the snack she was so ravenous for.

When she wasn't speaking in tongues, as he liked to joke, she kept her conversation as superficial as her smile. "I always loved the water, "or "I wish I lived in a log cabin" were some of the deepest thoughts she had expressed to him over the three years he had attempted to win her over. He held onto all of those little sentiments - to him, they were like keys to that cold steel buried deep in her chest.

As the seasons changed and countless attempts to kiss her were thwarted by a simple turn of her head, he began to straddle that fine line between hope and doubt. A nagging voice grew in the back of his mind telling him that he looked more like a fool than a white knight. Would this fair maiden rather stay locked in her tower than jump to the horse he had stationed below her castle walls? He questioned his love, and even wondered if it had been simple lust all along.

Regardless, he built her that log cabin in secret. He selected a piece of land on the edge of a cliff overlooking the water in his foggy port city town. The industrialized eastern section of the city broke off to a subdivision, aptly named "Red Head" for a large rock formation that, from certain angles, resembled a weathered man's face. The red rock stood resistant to the harsh elements, just as he continued to stand opposed to the cruel nature inherent to loving Emily Jane.

The log cabin was one of those prefabricated

cookie-cutter type homes. The wood was stained and sealed to keep it from decomposing. Its protective armour made it look more orange than you would have expected out of authentic wood. It had green shutters that adorned the windows to match the tin roof he paid handsomely for. He was proud of his offering, although he wished he had been handy enough to take the care and artisanship required to truly build a house with his bare hands rather than his wallet. His meticulous nature faded as he let a crew of men finish what he had started.

He scoured the adjacent beach for shells and sea glass and anything else that would make the faux natural homestead feel more authentic. The day before he was to unveil his labour of love, he pulled a large, twisted piece of driftwood from the sand near the Ducks Unlimited beach. It was smooth and grey and worn from its battle with the rough waters of the bay. He thought it was the perfect centerpiece to sit upon the mantle above the fireplace. It was almost faultless - with the exception of a spot of rot residing at the centre of its base. He dragged it back to the cabin and sanded the wood for hours that night, but the black core remained. The rot had made its way throughout the entire "perfect" piece of wood. The way it twisted and turned, and the smooth exterior had him awestruck despite the glaring blackness that resided within it. From the right angle, the rot could not be seen; its external beauty easily made up for its deficiency. He gave up trying to mend his showpiece and set it on the mantle, looking radiant, nonetheless.

His once-a-week date night arrived, and he placed a blindfold over her eyes. He had picked her up at the Island View Motel - the place she had worked since he had met her. He stumbled in one night after his friend Tom's bachelor party 3 years ago. The ladies at the strip club had gotten him hot and bothered and there she was working at the front desk, her blue eyes shining beneath the terrible fluorescent lighting, her top three buttons undone, revealing just enough of her breasts to leave him wanting more. She had that goofy smiling mask on, as she always did. When he asked her for her number that night, she laughed and rolled her eyes. He would have retired to his room to sleep off his drunken stupor if not for the way she followed it up with a seductive "come and get me" look that had him continue the chase.

"What if you don't like what you get?" she asked when she finally slid him her number. He never gave it another thought: how could he not like what he got with Emily Jane?

She sat in the passenger seat, blindfolded and smiling. The slow roaring moan tires make on a gravel driveway let her know that they had left the main roads.

"You silly boy," she said as his car rolled to a stop. She was giggling now.

"What?" he replied, puzzled. He had become accustomed to her weird sense of humor, but she had never called him that before.

"I can smell the ocean," she stated, ignoring his question. He had become accustomed to her deflecting his questions as well.

He turned off the car and didn't say another word. Getting out and walking to the passenger door, he reached out, grabbed her hand, and helped her to a standing position. Her hand felt cold in his clammy palm. Gripping her shoulders lightly, he walked behind her, noticing how stiff she was. His heart raced from the excitement, ready to unveil his gift to her.

He felt her arms move upwards, breaking his embrace as she pulled down the purple tie, ruining his surprise.

"I knew it. You silly boy," she said again, this time with the largest smile he'd ever seen on her face. She turned and hugged him. It was not the passionate kiss he was hoping for. It stung, but he remained composed.

"This isn't a real log cabin. You know that, George," she stated as a matter of fact. She burst out laughing and pulled him close for another hug. He put on the mask of a smiling face, but inside his heart broke.

He took her by the hand, and by the light of the harvest moon, led her to the log cabin. A thick heavy fog had rolled in from the Atlantic, typical for this time of year. It was fitting for such a somber occasion. His excitement had been drained from her lack of care at what he had done for her, drained from her response, and drained from 3 years he now felt had been wasted. His view of their relationship washed out as he recognized how fruitless his final act had become, buried beneath his own great expectations.

It was cold and dark inside; the scuttling of their feet echoed loudly within the hollow home. Her smile faded to that blank stare as she stood in the doorway with him. He left her side and walked towards the fireplace to start a fire for the evening. *You silly boy* echoed in his head as he lit some newspaper beneath the kindling. A fire roared to life and the living room was illuminated.

Sniffing the air, the stench of death stung his nostrils as he rose. A knot in his stomach cinched tight as he looked around the room. The orange wood interior was now black and brown. Rot had set in. He looked towards his perfect piece of driftwood. A blackened atrocity sat on the now rotten fireplace. The decay from within its core infected all of the surrounding wood. It seemed to move on its own, changing what was once shiny and new into a perversion of its previous form. The blackness engulfed the entire room and crept its way across the ceiling towards the front door as if it were filled with purpose. He could hear mumbling coming from where he left her. George stood there, numb, the knight in shining armour asleep at his post. He stared at the source of the disease on the fireplace in a daze. He caught his reflection in the mirror behind his rotten gift just as the loud clap of a door being slammed diverted his attention back to where he had left Emily Jane.

He could see her black outline standing by the door, her silhouette cast by the moonlight coming through a window. At the same time, her silhouette wavered in the light thrown by the flames to his rear. Her footsteps echoed loudly, mixing with her mumbling chant as she walked towards him in the rotting living room. His sweat streamed in beads down his horrified and embarrassed face. Her laugh filled the hollow cabin, a laugh more sinister and deeper than he had ever heard from her slender frame. The chant slowed and he could make out the words: "*stultus puer es animae tuae comedant*."

"You silly boy," it cackled in a horrendously unnatural growl as it wrung its bony fingers together. Her blonde hair was white and thin, and revealed balding patches on a withered head dripping with a black and brown slime. Her once blue eyes were now black and glassy, reflecting the fire's light. An emaciated and elongated torso covered in black scales stood there on thin legs. Broken wings dragged behind the thing Emily Jane had become.

The claws on its webbed feet pierced the floor as it stopped in front of him. Those black scales ran down across sagging breasts that hung on each side of an opened rib cage that exposed its dark insides. A blackened heart sat within its chest, as still as a broken watch. A smile sat on its face, larger than one could ever dream, exposing teeth jagged and broken, dripping with black ooze. He closed his eyes as he pictured Emily Jane's smiling face.

....

His screams went unheard, and his actions were met with disregard by the creature as it dug its cold hands through his hardened ribs. Penetrating his bleeding heart, it smiled, and laughed, playing with him until it had enough.

Leaving the log cabin, it slithered to the beach, disappearing into the frigid Atlantic waters.

Manufactured by Amazon.ca
Bolton, ON

35375749R00146